The D

Jeff Ross

orca sports

ORCA BOOK PUBLISHERS

Library and Archives Canada Cataloguing in Publication

Ross, Jeff, 1973-
The drop / Jeff Ross.
(Orca sports)

Issued also in electronic format.
ISBN 978-1-55469-392-4

I. Title. II. Series: Orca sports
PS8635.O6928D76 2011   JC813'.6   C2010-908000-9

First published in the United States, 2011
Library of Congress Control Number: 2010942089

Summary: When Alex and three other snowboarders find themselves in trouble
in the remote mountains of British Columbia, Alex must confront his fears
and lead them to safety.

Mixed Sources
Product group from well-managed forests,
controlled sources and recycled wood or fiber
www.fsc.org Cert no. SW-COC-000952
© 1996 Forest Stewardship Council

*Orca Book Publishers is dedicated to preserving the environment and has printed
this book on paper certified by the Forest Stewardship Council®.*

Orca Book Publishers gratefully acknowledges the support for its publishing
programs provided by the following agencies: the Government of Canada
through the Canada Book Fund and the Canada Council for the Arts, and the
Province of British Columbia through the BC Arts Council and
the Book Publishing Tax Credit.

Typesetting by Christine Toller
Cover photography by Getty Images
Author photo by Simon Bell

ORCA BOOK PUBLISHERS   ORCA BOOK PUBLISHERS
PO Box 5626, Stn. B   PO Box 468
Victoria, BC Canada   Custer, WA USA
V8R 6S4   98240-0468

www.orcabook.com
Printed and bound in Canada.

14 13 12 11 • 4 3 2 1

To Megan, for her patience.
To my parents, who always let me have
"just one more run," and to my kids.

chapter one

The helicopter pitched forward, almost tossing me out the open door. I grabbed the safety handle and pushed my goggles down over my eyes. There was a tap on my back. I turned around to see Dave waving at me to get out. In the front of the chopper, the copilot was making little circular motions with his hand. I knew what that meant: jump. The wind tossed the helicopter around and threw pellets of snow that felt like gravel on my face.

I shifted my snowboard away from where I had it wedged against the door. The helicopter jerked backward again, and I held on to the safety handle with all my strength.

"Take a deep breath," our instructor, Sam, said into my ear. I turned to look at him, and he smiled his big white smile. "Now exhale." I nodded. "And then you just float out." His hand drifted before him like a feather falling to earth. I nodded again. Inhaled, like he had told me.

Exhaled.

"Go, Alex," Dave shouted. Dave had been heli-boarding half a dozen times. This was the first time I had ever even *been* in a helicopter.

Never mind jumping out of one.

I inched my board forward and let it dangle over the edge. The ground was thick and white, like a giant duvet. The rotor blades of the helicopter forced the snow up and out. It seemed like I was about to fall into a cloud. I wanted to jump, but you know what they say—the first step is the hardest.

I inhaled again.

Exhaled.

Then I jumped.

It felt like I was falling forever. When my board finally touched down, I bent my knees to soften the impact. It still made my spine shake and sent a shiver through my entire body. But at least I was on the ground. The helicopter was floating above one of the highest peaks in British Columbia, far from the lift lines and groomed trails of Whistler Mountain. The powder was so deep here that there wasn't even a chance that the helicopter could land. So you had to jump.

I hopped a couple of times to get going. Then I leaned into the downhill and pushed hard to break free from the tornado-like conditions.

When I came out the other side of the whirlwind of snow, the world was bright blue and glaring white. I could see forever. In the distance, other peaks poked into the clouds. I had never been up this high on a mountain before. I did two quick turns, dug in hard on my toe edge and settled in beside Bryce and Hope, two of the other Backcountry Patrol hopefuls.

"What took you so long?" Hope asked.

"My board got caught on the door."

The little bit of Hope's face that wasn't covered by pink tuque, goggles or neck warmer screwed up in a familiar way. "You mean you got scared."

I pointed at the front of my board. "It got stuck on the doorframe. I had to get it out. I didn't want to scrape up the bottom."

"Seriously, Alex, how many rails did you do yesterday?" she said. "And now you want me to believe you are suddenly all concerned about the bottom of your board?"

I had spent the last two weeks training with Dave, Hope and Bryce. Dave was arrogant, but he didn't have the skills to back up his talk. Bryce was the best nonprofessional snowboarder I had ever seen. When the rest of us were making big jumpy turns down the hill, Bryce was cutting smooth lines. He was good— great even. But it was nothing to him.

Just something he could do. Hope was... well, I don't even know how to explain what Hope was. First off, she's a girl. Not that I think girls shouldn't be Backcountry Patrollers—just not *this* girl. I could only imagine what she would do if she found someone half dead in the woods or caught on a ledge. My guess was that, at best, she might become a groomed-slope Ski Patroller. Which, as far as I was concerned, was about the worst thing you could be.

"Believe whatever you want, Hope." I knelt down on the ground, my board out behind me, and let the cool breeze rush across my face. The helicopter was pitching in the wind. It went forward, then back, then a little higher, then down so low that it almost touched the ground. Suddenly Dave dropped out of the side of the helicopter and disappeared into the tornado of snow. A moment later he was beside us, wiping snow from his goggles.

"Nice one," Bryce said. Dave nodded as though he already knew it had been a nice jump. The helicopter pitched back again,

5

then lifted up another twenty feet off the ground. "What's happening?" I asked. Sam, our instructor and lone connection to the rest of the world, was still on board.

"He said he'd be right behind me," Dave said. We watched as the helicopter rose again, higher into the endless sky.

"He can't just leave us," Hope said.

"Maybe it's part of the test," Bryce said.

"Leaving us on the side of the mountain?" Hope said. "Alone? That is *not* what I signed up for." The chopper lifted slightly, and Sam slid out the open door. He fell for a moment and then grabbed the landing skid. He did a couple of quick chin-ups, held the back edge of his board with one hand and let go of the skid.

He seemed to fall in slow motion, twisting at the same time. Just before he hit the ground, he kicked the board out and disappeared from view. It was like watching an Olympic high diver.

Beautiful.

"What was that?" Bryce said, obviously impressed.

"Wow," Dave said, giving his head a little shake. Fifteen years ago, Sam Jenkins had been considered the best snowboarder on the planet. He had been the first professional boarder to do a 900 in a half-pipe during competition. That's two and a half *full* turns in the air. And this was back in the days when snowboards were so long and heavy that it took an amazing amount of strength just to launch yourself into the air. But Sam was one of those people who seemed to defy gravity. He was on the cover of magazines and won or placed in every competition he entered. There was even an early video of him and another pro boarder, Mike Carolina, tackling a hill that skiers had all but given up on.

Then one day he and Mike Carolina disappeared.

No one knew where they had gone. People said they were traveling the globe, looking for the highest peaks. The most extreme verts. Others thought they'd turned their talents to surfing and were in Australia or Hawaii riding waves. But no one really knew. Now Mike Carolina was still missing, and Sam was the man who would decide whether we would become Backcountry Patrollers and work the back hills of British Columbia, or if we would be shuffled over to the Ski Patrol. The difference between the two was night and day. Ski Patrollers ride lifts all day, warn people not to stand around in certain spots, and pick little kids up off the bunny slopes. Maybe, just *maybe,* now and then Ski Patrollers have to go off trail to drag someone out of the bush. Backcountry Patrol was something different altogether.

Something brand-new.

Backcountry Patrollers had nothing to do with groomed slopes and bunny trails. They were sent in when someone got into trouble while skiing or snowboarding in the backcountry. Until now, it had always been a job for skiers accompanied by snow-mobiles. But last winter a snowboarder had managed to get into and out of the bush and save a woman who had gone off a cliff where no one else—not skiers or snowmobilers—had been able to do a thing. We'd been told early on that only one or two of us would be selected to work with the Backcountry Patrol. If we passed these tests, our job would be to help people who were in serious danger.

Our job would be to save lives.

"Where'd he go?" Bryce asked now. We were huddled behind a large outcropping. The helicopter had lifted off and disappeared into the clouds that almost touched the top of this peak.

It was silent and cold. Colder than I thought it would be. And with the helicopter gone, all I could hear was the wind rushing across the blank white space.

"Well, he has to be somewhere. He couldn't just *disappear*," Hope said. Bryce took a couple of jumps toward the little ledge behind us. His goggles shone in the bright sunlight. It was a beautiful sunny day. But there were dark clouds in the distance.

"There he is," Bryce said. Sam looked like a child, waving at us from the bottom of four fairly big drops. Our two-way radios crackled.

"All right, guys," Sam's voice came through, muffled and tossed around by the wind. "Time for your first test. Over."

Dave grabbed his radio and raised it to his face. "How did you get down there? Over."

"I rode my board, David. Now it's time to see what you four have in you. And since you just volunteered, David, you can go first. Over."

"Where? Over."

"Down here. Four easy drops," Sam said. "The first two are about ten feet, maybe twelve. The third is only five or six and the final one...Well, you'll see. Over." Sam insisted we finish all our communications with "Over."

Dave turned to us. He wore these giant goggles and his hat down low, but his lips quivered, and he mashed a gloved hand on the back of his head whenever he was nervous. Which was often. "Bryce should go first," Dave said. "He's already at the edge." There was nothing from the radio. "Sam?" No response. "Sam?" Dave looked more worried.

"Are we missing something here, David? Over." Sam sounded irritated.

Dave shook his head. "Bryce should go first. He's on the edge already. Over."

"Fine. Bryce, would you like to go first? Over," Sam said. Bryce jumped off the ledge he was perched on and shot down the side of the mountain without a word. "I'll take that as a yes. Over."

It was an impressive run. First he cut around an outcropping, and then he spun into an open space and aimed himself toward the drops. Everything he did was compact and tight. There didn't seem to be a single wasted movement.

"Your turn, David. Over," Sam said. Dave nodded a couple of times. He put the radio in his pocket and then pulled it out again.

"Any hints, Bryce? Over," he said. His hand was shaking.

"Just hit them straight. Maybe pull back a little before the third one or you'll have

11

too much speed for the last one," Bryce said. The radio crackled off, then back on again. "Oh. Over." Dave put the radio back in his pocket and made a big production of zipping it up.

"Just go, Dave," Hope said.

"I'm going. I'm going."

"Then goooooooo."

Dave patted himself down one last time. Then he jumped over the side of the ledge.

His run was awkward. He slowed almost to a stop just before each drop and then kind of fell over the side. He always landed on his board, although after the second drop, he had to jump a couple of times to get going again.

It wasn't pretty. But he got to the end of it and settled in beside Sam and Bryce.

"All right, Alex. Your turn. Over," Sam said. I didn't even bother to respond. I just jumped, twisted my board in the air and pushed hard toward the first drop.

chapter two

I tried to follow Bryce's line down the slope. But by the time I got to the first drop, I was going way too fast. I stuttered, dug deep with my heel edge, then twisted back, head-on to the drop and sailed off. "Bend your knees," I told myself as I landed. Powder flew everywhere. I cut a little farther than Bryce's line and straightened out for the second drop. It came faster than I had expected, but I managed to get squared to it and keep the front tip of my board up as I dropped off. I went toe edge, leaning forward, and did a nice slow arc. Flipped to my heel edge, leaning way back as the board dug into the powder, and aimed at the third drop. It was easy enough. Not even really a drop, but more of a steep incline.

Then came the fourth drop.

It didn't look like anything until I noticed the lip on it. It was like a launch pad. I tried to crouch when I hit it to lessen the amount of air I got, but it was impossible. I sailed off, and my board got kind of wobbly beneath me. I reached down, grabbed the back side of my board, right between my heels. Just before I landed, I gave it a little twist. Flair, you know. Style.

I did a couple of quick turns in the deep powder. Then I carved up and around to where the others stood.

"Nice," Sam said. "But tricks are not appreciated out here. Remember?"

"It wasn't really a trick," I said. "I had to stabilize my board and..." Sam waved a hand at me, all the while looking up the mountain. His blond curls flipped out beneath his tuque. His eyes were hidden behind a pair of sunglasses, but I knew they were an icy blue. I couldn't think of a time I'd ever seen him wear goggles. He tilted the glasses down a little and looked at me.

"It's all right out here today. But think about this when you're on Backcountry Patrol. You do a trick, jam yourself up, and you're done. So is whoever you were sent out to save. Cool?"

"Cool," I replied. I turned away from the rest of them as a giddy grin crossed my face. Sam had said *when* you're on Backcountry Patrol. Not *if,* but *when.*

We all looked uphill to where Hope stood. She was all pink. A maddening pink. A bright, glowing pink blob of cotton candy caught on the side of the mountain. Even her board, an evo 5150, and bindings were pink. I mean, you can like a color and all, but seriously. Mix it up a little.

Sam pulled out his two-way and spoke into it.

15

"All right, girl, your go. Show us your stuff. Over." There was no response. "Hope? Over." Again, no response. He turned to me. "Did she have her radio on?" I shrugged. "Hope can you hear me? Over."

"Yeah," came her little voice.

"Yeah what? Over."

"Yeah. Over."

"Better. It's your go. Over." Sam let his arm drop by his side. He was moving his gloved thumb up and down the radio.

"She's scared," Dave said. Bryce picked up his radio and held it to his face.

"Hope, you there? Over."

"Yeah. Over."

"It's nothing. Three little drops. The fourth one has a lip on it, so bend your knees when you hit it. That way you'll absorb it and not get launched. No problem. Over." There was no response.

"Oh man, we're going to be out here all day waiting for her to go," Dave said. The sun was getting higher and warming the air. It was almost noon, and the clouds that had been pushing in on us seemed to be heading south. It was still cold, but nice to feel the sunshine.

The pom-pom on Hope's tuque suddenly jumped into the air. A moment later she was cutting a large half circle toward the first drop. It looked good. She was following the line Dave had taken. Just before the first drop, she kicked out twice on her toe side and drifted slowly toward the edge. She dropped over much like I had, though she didn't bend her knees. The impact actually caused her to pick up more speed, and suddenly she was shooting toward the second drop. She came off it straight, landed flat, wobbled and got up on her toe side again. It looked like she was going to wipe out off the third drop. Somehow she managed to get herself straight enough to float over. Then she aimed herself at the final drop. She was heading straight at it, bent down, in perfect position to launch. But instead of holding this pose, she suddenly slid sideways, and hit the lip at a bit of an angle. She got huge air, floating up and out farther than any of the rest of us had. The only problem was that she was sideways to the hill. Land like that, and it isn't just doing a face-plant you have to worry about. I cringed, not really wanting to see what was going to happen next.

Just as Hope was about to hit the ground, she suddenly yanked herself around and landed backward to the slope. Now riding backward down the hill, she had to push hard on her tip to swing the board up and around. She did this with more grace than I thought she possessed, then swept in toward us, spraying everyone with snow before falling into a heap.

"What was *that*?" Dave said.

"I got twisted," she said.

"That was pretty cool," Bryce said. Hope smiled and reached an arm out. Bryce leaned forward and pulled her to her feet. Sam looked at her for a moment, then turned his attention to the top of the mountain. He pushed his sunglasses back up his nose.

"When you get into these things, you just have to do it. You know what I mean?" Sam said. He seemed to be talking more to the mountain than us. "Sure, you have to be cautious if you're the first one in. But I was already down here. I let you know what it was going to be like. You all have the skills to pull off something like this. You *know* you have the skills. You wouldn't *be* here if you didn't have the skills. So believe in yourselves and just go."

I looked up at the sky to where Sam's attention seemed to be stuck. Two minutes before, it had been a beautiful day. Now, the dark clouds that had been heading south were rolling back over us. We were so high up and they were so low, it seemed like we could touch them.

Sam smiled, nodding his head. "We're standing on the top of the world here. It doesn't get much better than this." He slapped his hands together and looked at us. "All right. There were supposed to be two more tests to do here, but I don't like the look of those clouds. The last thing we want is to be stuck out here in a storm. So let's only do one of the tests and then get into the cabin in case bad weather hits."

"What are we going to do?" Dave asked. He looked scared already.

"See the trees down there?" Sam pointed to a little forest beneath us. It was strange to see growth so high up. But I guess it was flat enough that things just grew. "There's an object in there you have to find. First one to do so gets a prize."

"What kind of object?" Dave asked.

"What kind of prize?" Bryce said.

Sam shook his head. "That would just be giving it all away, wouldn't it?" He straightened himself to the hill. "Stay to the right of me, all right?"

"Sure," I said. "Why?"

He pointed to the left. "Dead Man's Drop. Ever heard of it?" We all shook our heads. "It's some kind of geological freak show over there. There are spots where the drop to the other side is no more than three or four feet. But in other places there's a slit in the mountain that goes all the way to the bottom."

"What do you mean, all the way to the bottom?" Bryce asked.

"The bottom of the mountain. Hundreds of feet straight down."

"Whatever," Hope said. "That's not even, like, possible."

"All right," Sam replied, "don't believe me. But stay in the bush anyway, okay?"

"How come no one knows where it's four feet and where it's five hundred feet?" Hope asked.

"Because the snow swirls around there all the time. Wind or no wind, it's like waves breaking on the shore. I know a spot or two where it might not be that big a drop, but then, you can't be certain." Hope must have looked at him as though she thought he was full of it. "No, that's all right. No one believes me. Cool, cool. But still, stay to the right." He jumped a couple of times and started shooting down the hill. "Remember"—his voice floated back—"first one to find the mystery object gets a prize!" The four of us looked at one another and then, all at once, jumped and tucked down the incline toward the forest.

chapter three

By the time we got to the lightly forested area, the clouds had closed in above us and a vicious wind had picked up. Bryce was the first into the woods, cutting far to the right and shooting between a couple of saplings. Hope followed closely behind. Dave went for the middle, which was likely the smart choice. I steered over to where Sam was leaning against a tree. Then I cut back toward the middle. I figured there must be a reason for him to be standing where he was. Maybe it was even a clue as to where the object was.

Boarding through trees is about the worst thing you can do. I mean, short of dropping off a two-hundred-foot cliff or something stupid like that. Snowboarders need a little more space to turn than skiers do. As for stopping, well, that's another story altogether. You can't just snowplow your way to a stop in trees. Once stopped, however, you can very easily hop from one spot to another or pull yourself up with branches. But most of all, since you aren't holding on to poles, your hands are completely free. You see a lot of Ski Patrollers without poles. But they tend to be holding on to something—a sled or a first-aid kit— and they look really awkward. Boarders never look awkward.

At least I don't think so.

After about two minutes, I discovered that I had taken a difficult line. It was tight in there, and the trees were all bunched together. There was the odd old-growth oak or spruce, but generally it was little saplings that whipped my face or snagged under the board and shot me sideways. I caught an edge as I was about to pivot around a very large tree. I stumbled, righted myself and dug in hard on the back edge of my board, trying to turn. I wasn't really thinking about anything more than *not* hitting that tree.

The tree near Dead Man's Drop.

I busted out of the woods and found myself on a thin stretch of open space. The powder was deep, and after coming out of the fairly low snow of the forested area, it felt like I'd been shot straight into the middle of a huge bowl of ice cream. I leaned back, as you have to in deep powder, and tried to do a bounce turn. I wanted to stop, but I knew if I did, it would be really, *really* hard to get going again.

The bounce turn sent me up into the air. I kicked out and landed on my toe side, cutting softly back toward the forested area. There seemed to be hundreds of saplings in front of me. I didn't really feel like getting beat up again by them. So I shifted back onto my heel, trying another turn in the deep powder. It felt good. Actually, it felt amazing. It was everything I had ever wanted from life, right there.

Then I saw the snow squall along the edge of what had to be Dead Man's Drop. Sam was right. It looked like waves crashing on a shore. The snow would come up, shoot straight into the air, then fall back down along the edge of the drop. There was no way of telling how much of a fall it was. A hissing, howling sound accompanied the squall. It sounded like voices, like people moaning down there. I stared for too long, and by the time I thought to watch where I was going, I was almost to the edge. I dug in hard on my toe side and put my right arm down on the top of the powder to turn as quickly and tightly as possible. The waves of the drop brushed over me, covering my goggles with a thin wash of snow. I brought my left hand around to try and wipe it away. When I could see clearly again, I was about five feet from a tree. I had no choice. I bailed.

Hard.

I came to an abrupt stop face-first in the powder, my board spinning out above me and bending my legs. I pushed my hands down and tried to roll over, but the snow just gave way. I sank deeper. I could still breathe, but it was getting harder. The snow was light and fluffy on the surface, but when it was pounded down, it became as solid as concrete. Everything was dark. I shook my head and tried to think. We'd been taught what to do in a situation like this. My training came back. Sam's voice in my head. "Get on your back. The last thing you want is to feel like you're in a coffin. Look at the sky." But how? How do you go from being facedown in the snow to lying on your back? I tried twisting, but that didn't work. So I jammed my board down until it stayed steady. Then I rolled myself over.

There was no sky. Just darkness.

The clouds had settled in, and everything above the trees was black. To my left, the horrible moaning from the drop continued. Snow shot up into the sky. It truly was a terrifying place.

I started pumping my legs, trying to get my board underneath me. The sooner I got away from here, I thought, the better.

The trees to my right bent under the press of the wind. I tried to slow my breath and calm down. Panicking here could be deadly. I pushed my hands into the snow, but this just made me sink deeper. I sat still for a minute and looked at the cold, dark sky. I wasn't going to get lost out here. If I was going to be a Backcountry Patroller, I had to be brave enough to get myself out of this kind of predicament. I wiggled my legs until I got my board free and beneath me. Then, in one quick motion, I stood up.

The wind blew ice into my face. It felt terrible. Like a thousand bees stinging all at once. Now that my face was wet from the snow, it felt even worse. I had to get somewhere warmer quickly or risk serious frostbite on my face. I took a last glance behind me at the rolling, churning wash of the drop. Then I jumped as hard as I could, kicking snow from the top of my board, and cut back into the woods.

It was quieter there. I took some deep breaths and tried to stay as horizontal to the slope as possible. I wasn't at all worried about finding the object or winning the prize. I just wanted to get out of there and inside the warm cabin. Maybe listen to some music to get the terrible sound of the drop out of my ears.

I had traveled halfway across the wooded area when I came to a clearing. It was almost peaceful in this little square where no trees had found root. The sun filled the space with heat. I turned from my toe side to my heel and cut along the tree line, looking for a place to drop into the deeper woods, finally comfortable being surrounded by trees. There was a bit of a chute ahead of me. Maybe ten feet between trees. As far as I could see, this kept up for the rest of the wooded area. I steered toward it. And then, just as I was about to go onto my front edge again and drop into the chute,

I spotted something leaned up against a tree. At first I couldn't tell what it was. A lump of blue and orange fabric, like a jacket left outside through a long winter. Then I got closer, and I could see exactly what it was.

A person. A big person.

chapter four

My heart jumped in my chest. I swung around the tree until I was right beside the body. Its head was tilted forward and down. Its arms hung limp at its sides. I couldn't see skis or a snowboard. Just a jacket and snow. How long had he been out here? Was no one looking for him? I got a little closer and thought about checking for a pulse or something, but it was too much.

Way too much.

So I just started yelling.

"Help, help! Over here. There's a guy. Help." No one came. I had totally forgotten about the two-way radio. "Come on, man, get up. Just stand up and walk away from this," I said. I was beginning to wonder if he was alive. The jacket was so puffy, I couldn't tell if he was breathing. He didn't move. I yelled again, but no one responded or swept in to help. It was all up to me.

I took a glove off and reached my hand out. I forced myself to move my hand past the collar of his jacket and beneath his neck warmer. His skin was cold and spongy. I yanked my hand out, hitting his goggles on the way past. They fell to the ground, and his dead eyes stared back at me. But something wasn't right. His eyes looked dead, for sure, but his eyebrows were strange. As if they were painted on. And his nose was deformed—hacked off at the end. Yet there was no blood.

I reached out and lifted his tuque. His hair was painted on as well. He had no ears. No mouth. Just a painted on slit. Everything was fake because *he* was fake.

A dummy.

The two-way radio snapped to life.

"Did you find Keith Richards? Over." Sam's voice.

Was he nuts? "Who the hell is Keith Richards? Over."

"The Rolling Stones? You seriously don't know who the Stones are? Over."

"What is this about, Sam? Over."

"You found the object, Alex. Congrats, man. Over."

"The object? Over."

"Yeah. The prize is yours. Over."

"And what would that prize be? Over."

"You get to carry Keith Richards down to the cabin. Over," Sam said.

I looked at the mass of plastic I'd thought was a person. "I have to carry a dummy down to the cabin? Over."

"Alex, Alex. Please don't call Keith a dummy, it's not nice. Over."

The wind roaring up the chute was cold and deafening. The button keeping one of my pant legs tight across my boot had popped off and was waving in the breeze, leaving my ankle to freeze. I took my other glove off and tried to fix it.

"You still there, Alex? Over."

"Yeah, I'm still here. How am I supposed to carry this thing? Over."

"That's for you to decide. But be gentle. As you can see, Keith's been through a lot recently. Over." I got my pant leg secured over my boot. Then I pulled the dummy out of the snow. He was heavy. An absolute deadweight. At least he didn't have a board on. In fact, he didn't even have legs.

"Oh, and Alex? Over."

"What? Over." I had lifted the dummy up and had to drop him back down again to push the button on the radio.

"You scream like a little girl. Over."

I flicked the radio off and put it back in my pocket. It took me a minute to figure it out, but finally I decided that putting the dummy on my back and tying the sleeves of his jacket over one shoulder and under the other arm would likely do the trick. He was heavy, and it felt strange once I got him attached.

Every time I shifted from heel to toe, he flung out beside me, throwing me completely off balance. I looked down the long chute out of the woods and wondered just how far away the cabin was.

chapter five

"Keith!" Sam yelled when I stepped in the door of the cabin. It was just after three o'clock. It had taken me over an hour of falling, swearing and heaving the stupid dummy to get to the cottage. A journey that likely took the rest of the Backcountry Patrol hopefuls about fifteen minutes.

I dropped the dummy on the ground, face-first, and stepped on him.

"Have some respect," Sam said. "The man is an artist."

"What's he talking about?" Dave said. He and Hope and Bryce were seated around a table, steaming bowls of stew in front of them.

"Yeah, Alex, what's going on?" Bryce asked. "Sam said you won the prize, but he wouldn't tell us anything else."

I gave Keith Richards a kick in the head. Then I walked across the room to where a woodstove was pumping out heat. "The object," I said, "was that. A dummy."

"Ahh, man, what did I say about that? He's no dummy." Sam had gathered the dummy up in his arms and was cradling it like a baby.

"The prize was carrying that stupid thing all the way down here," I continued. Sam placed the dummy in a chair, stroked his painted-on hair and shook his head.

"Who told you that?" Sam said.

"You did."

"I said no such thing. I said you'd found the object. I said you screamed like a girl. But I never said carrying Keith Richards was the prize."

I knelt in front of the stove and rubbed my hands together. I was sure some part of me must have frostbite. Maybe a few parts. But I wouldn't know which ones until I started to thaw.

"So what *is* the prize?" Dave asked.

Sam smiled. "Alex doesn't have to haul Keith down the mountain tomorrow."

"Great prize," I said. "Seeing as I just *did* that."

"Ahhh, but you see, it is. Because tomorrow these three"—he gestured at Hope, Bryce and Dave—"will be carrying the Jonas Brothers downhill. And those three are certainly dummies. The plan for tomorrow is as follows." Sam turned to the other three. "I will go out early and hide the Jonas bothers. You will go out and find them." Sam went to a built-in closet and opened the door. Three identical dummies hung from hooks. It was kind of spooky. "When you each find your victim, you will perform CPR. Then you will carry your victim to a designated location farther down the mountain. A spot, I will add, that is double the distance Alex just carried Keith Richards here." Sam slammed the closet door and sat down beside Keith Richards.

"That's not fair," Hope said immediately. "They look really heavy. I mean, I'll try to carry one, but..."

"They are heavy," Sam said. "Well, not *that* heavy. Not as heavy as a real person. Likely half the weight of anyone you'd ever have to haul off this mountain, unless garden gnomes suddenly take up extreme sports."

"I still don't know if I'll be able to carry that kind of weight," Hope said.

"And *I* know you can." Sam tapped his head. "It's all in your head. If you know you can do something, you can."

"The heaviest thing I have ever carried on a board was that stretcher last week with the first-aid kit." Hope looked worried. She stuck a finger in her mouth and started chewing the nail. "Carrying one of those dummies all the way down the hill. That's tough..."

Sam stared at her for a moment, then grabbed a large satellite cell phone off the table beside him and began pressing buttons.

"What are you doing?" Hope asked.

"Calling base camp. I'll have them send a chopper up in the morning to get you out of here."

"Why? What did I do?"

"If you can't carry one of the Jonas Brothers down the mountain, then you may as well quit now."

"But what if I ca...?" Hope's voice trailed off.

Sam put the phone back on the table and glared at Hope. "What did I tell you last week about that sentence? Huh? Anyone?"

"If you say you can't," Bryce said, "you won't."

Sam pointed a finger at him.

"Exactly. Say you can't and—guess what?—you can't. That simple. So, Hope, if you want to give up, give up. Drop out. Go home. It's fine with me. I can put in a recommendation to the lift operators or, I don't know, maybe the Baby Bushwhackers.

You can help five-year-olds bang into poles all day."

"No way. I'm going to be a Backcountry Patroller," Hope said.

Sam stood up quickly and crossed the room. He grabbed a free chair and banged it on the floor a couple of times. He seemed to be overreacting. I had no idea why. Hope had really just been thinking out loud. A little encouragement likely would have been a better idea.

"Then act like one!" Sam yelled. "Say I pass you. I mean, dream with me here. Say I pass you, and you end up being in Backcountry Patrol and you're out here one day alone."

"Backcountry Patrollers never work alone," Hope said.

"All right," Sam said, a bit more calmly. "You're out with a partner and you're looking for someone who has gone down and hurt himself. Then your partner—*whoosh*—over an edge." Sam sent a hand out before him and fluttered it off a make-believe cliff. "Now you're alone and you have to carry some guy down the mountain. If you don't get to him and help him, he will die. Would that be fair to him?"

Hope looked into the murky depths of her stew.

"Would it?" Sam yelled.

"No."

"No. Exactly. So, if you can't do it, then don't. We'll get a chopper here for you. But if you want to be in Backcountry Patrol, then say you *can* do it. And go out there in the morning and do it." Sam banged the chair on the floor one last time, then stormed off into the bathroom.

"Wow," Dave said. "What was that all about?"

Hope looked like she was about to cry. I felt badly for her. Sam really seemed to have gone off the deep end for no reason.

She folded her napkin, picked up her half-eaten bowl of stew and dumped the remains into the garbage. Then she rinsed the bowl, set the spoon in the sink and went over to where her stuff was piled on the floor. We all watched her without saying a word. She pulled an iPod out of the bag, plugged the earbuds into her ears, climbed into a bright pink sleeping bag and turned her back to us.

"He's right, you know," Dave said in a quiet tone. "If you can't carry a dummy down the mountain, you're pretty much useless out here."

"He could have been a little kinder about it though," Bryce said.

"Why? If she can't do it, she can't do it. Better to get her out of here." Dave shook his head and jammed another spoonful of stew into his mouth. "What do you think, Alex?"

I took my jacket off and hung it on the back of the empty chair. I knew why Dave wanted Hope gone. It increased his chances of getting into Backcountry Patrol.

"I think...tomorrow, it's going to suck to be any of you," I said.

Dave looked angry, but Bryce started to laugh.

"Now, where's the rest of that stew?" I said. "I'm starving."

We finished eating and sat around the woodstove, talking. Sam came out of the bathroom and sat staring at the flames through the stove's glass front. Eventually we all got into our sleeping bags for the night. When everyone was lying down reading or listening to music, Sam went outside and came back smelling of alcohol. I'd seen him pull the little silver flask out of an inside pocket a few times during the past week. I didn't like the idea that Sam, our only link to civilization, was drinking. But what could I do?

"Someone has to feed the woodstove in the night," Sam said. "Alex has been through enough today. Dave helped me make dinner. So it's up to you, Bryce."

Bryce was on his bunk in his thermal wear, turning the wheel on his iPod.

"Okay."

"Set your alarm. By three AM the fire will be down to nothing. Get up, put four logs in, make sure they catch and then go back to bed."

"Okay."

"If the fire goes out, we will freeze. You understand that, right?"

"Yeah."

There were two oil lanterns lighting the room. One sat on the dining table and another hung from a rafter. Sam shut the door of the woodstove and then flicked the two lanterns off. The glow from our iPod screens was the only light in the room.

"Good night," Sam said. I plugged my earbuds in and settled on the song that had been stuck in my head all day long: Crowbar's "Oh, What a Feeling." It was old and corny, and people would probably make fun of me for listening to it. But it explained exactly how snowboarding made me feel.

I listened to it five times in a row before I fell asleep with the music still humming in my ears.

I woke once in the night to some banging. I opened my eyes. Everything was hazy. By the dim glow of the woodstove I could make out Bryce, wrapped in a blanket, staring into the depths of the flickering fire. I was going to say something, but I was too tired. I went back to sleep and dreamed about endless powder and peaks that tore holes in the sky.

chapter six

I woke up freezing. The room was still dark. I checked my watch: 6:00 AM. I rolled over and squinted into the dimness. Sam was trying to coax the fire back to life. He put a piece of paper onto a log and began blowing.

"Why is it so cold?" I said. Sam turned and looked at me. Even in the dim light, I could tell his eyes were bloodshot.

"Bryce didn't put enough logs on the fire last night," he replied. I looked over at Bryce's bunk. There was a lump there, but I couldn't see his head sticking out the top. Dave's tuque-covered head poked out of the top of his sleeping bag. I leaned over and looked down on Hope's bunk. It was a mess of pink. Sleeping bag, tuque, even the blanket. Our bags had been brought in by snowmobile the day before. We'd been told to pack as lightly as possible. I had a feeling that Hope hadn't listened to that advice. Her bag was huge. I have no idea what she'd stuffed in there, but it looked heavy, and she groaned every time she picked it up.

I swung myself out over the edge of the bunk and landed firmly on the ground. As I passed Bryce's sleeping bag, I punched the area where I figured his legs would be.

My fist went deep into nothing. I yanked the sleeping bag back and discovered that the lump was actually Keith Richards. "Sam, Bryce isn't here."

"What?" Sam leaned away from the stove and looked at me.

"He's not here. He's gone." A wicked wind howled outside, banging against the window and shaking the door.

"Where is he?" Sam said.

"I don't know," I replied. The bathroom door was closed. "Maybe he's in the bathroom."

I went over and knocked on the door. There was no answer, so I opened it and looked inside. It was a simple bathroom. Simple and empty. "He's not in here," I said.

"What?" Dave's sleepy voice came from across the room.

"Bryce is gone," I said.

"What? Where would he go?" Dave jumped out of bed.

"I don't know," I said.

Sam held his hands up, palms out, and said, "He likely went out to get a run in."

Dave's eyes went wide, and his voice was little more than a whisper. "It's still dark out. Where would he go? And what would he do when he got to the bottom of the run?"

Sam crossed the room and opened the door. Snow blew in, making a thin white blanket on the floor. He stuck his head out and looked left and right. Then he came back in and closed the door.

"His snowboard's here."

"What about the snowmobiles?" Two snowmobiles had been left for us to use during our training.

"Yeah," Sam said. "Still here. Both of them."

"So where did he go?" Dave yelled. "He couldn't just disappear!"

"Calm down," Sam said. "Let's all just calm down. I'm sure there's an explanation. I mean, people don't just disappear, right?"

"Who disappeared?" Hope's voice came from deep inside her sleeping bag.

"Bryce is gone," Dave replied. "Vanished."

"When I was over at the drop," I said, "there was...a sound. Like people moaning. Moaning and crying."

"You went near the drop?" Dave said.

"I got kicked out of the woods and ended up right next to it."

"So what are you saying?" Dave asked. He had taken his tuque off and his red hair stuck up on his head like flames "That something came and dragged him down there?"

"No. I mean...No, that's stupid."

"Exactly," Sam said. "Come on, Alex. What are you trying to do? Scare everybody? The wind always sounds like that at the drop." He reached up and lit the lantern over his head. The room suddenly filled with light.

"I don't know," I said. "I don't know. Where could he have gone? Are there footprints or anything?"

"No. Nothing." Sam pointed at the door. "It's a blizzard out there."

"We have to call someone," Dave yelled. He charged around the room, taking quick little steps. Sam grabbed him by the shoulders and held him steady.

"Dave, my man, I need you to calm down. All right? You hear me?"

Dave started shaking his head. "Where could he have gone?" Dave said. "No snowmobile. No board. How deep is the snow out there? Why would he go anywhere?"

"Maybe he felt badly about not putting enough logs in the stove," Hope suggested. "Maybe he's, like, I don't know, punishing himself?"

"That's stupid," Dave said. He had grabbed his jacket off the end of his bunk and put it on. Now, whenever he moved his arms, he made swishing sounds. It would have been funny in some other situation.

Sam went back to the woodstove and began blowing again. The room wasn't getting any warmer. I used the bathroom and then came back out and put on my jacket and snow pants. Sam had the satellite phone out and was waiting for it to find a signal.

"I'll call base camp," Sam said. "They can send a chopper up to help find him."

He seemed relieved at the possibility of getting help. He pressed the button on the phone again, waited and then pressed it again. He put the phone to his ear.

"What's going on?" Dave asked.

"It's not connecting," Sam replied.

This was bad.

We were a long way from anywhere, or anyone. Even if we made it to the bottom of the mountain, we were still a long way from any roads or towns. Without the satellite phone, we were on our own in the wild.

"There's a pickup spot though, right?" I said.

Sam shook his head. "It was to be arranged."

"Okay," I said. "But people know we are here. They know when we're supposed to get picked up, right?"

Sam shrugged. "I don't like to nail down the details. It's too much planning. Too many variables. I said three or four days. Everything depends on the weather."

"What about food?" Dave yelped. "How much food do we have?"

"Lots," Sam said. "Especially now that Bryce is gone." He laughed. No one else did. I went and looked out the window. It was pitch-dark.

Dave started laughing. We all looked at him. Red hair straight up in the air. Hands on his knees. Laughing.

"What?" I said.

"What?" Sam said.

"What are you laughing at?" Hope said.

Dave shook his head. "It's a test, isn't it?" Sam raised an eyebrow. "We have to go out there now and find Bryce. You've got him stashed in another hut somewhere nearby. He's fine. Just hidden. Another test, that's all."

"I wish that were the case, but it isn't," Sam said.

Dave's face fell. "So you really don't know where he is?"

"Not a clue."

"This isn't all a setup?" Dave said.

"No setup."

"Let me see the phone," Dave grabbed the phone out of Sam's hand and started pounding the power button.

"This isn't working," Dave said.

"That's what I told you," Sam said.

Dave sat down in a chair. "We're screwed," he said. "Screwed."

chapter seven

We couldn't do anything that morning. The storm was so wild, we could barely open the door, never mind step out. But then around noon, the clouds broke apart and the world suddenly seemed clear and pure. Nothing but deep white powder and high blue skies.

I stood at the doorway looking up at the sky. Our boards were covered in snow. I pulled mine out and brushed it off.

"Where are you going?" Hope asked.

"I don't know." I looked at the endless hills and trees around us. "He has
to be out here somewhere. He couldn't
just vanish."

"So, what? You're going to ride to the
bottom of the mountain? Get help? Save
everyone?" she said.

I looked behind Hope into the cabin.
Dave was jabbing the buttons on the
satellite phone, and Sam was standing over
him, looking expectantly at the screen.

"I don't know what I'm going to do,"
I said. "But I've got to do something."

Hope disappeared from the doorway
and came back a minute later in her jacket
and snow pants.

"Well, a board is going to be useless
here," she said.

"We can take the snowmobiles," I said.
I had only ever ridden on the back of a
snowmobile. The idea of starting one up
and driving it was a little frightening.
I was superaware that a fall could have me
tumbling and rolling down three hundred
feet. With a big machine on top of me.

"Wherever Bryce went, he went on foot."
I said. "His board is here. The snowmobiles
are here. So he couldn't have gone far."

I looked at the empty landscape. The
cabin was on a flat space. It was steep
above and below.

Dave suddenly appeared at the doorway.
"What are you guys doing?"

"We're going to go find Bryce," Hope
said. The keys were in the snowmobiles.
She brushed the snow off the seat of one
of them, sat down and turned the key. The
snowmobile roared to life. Hope unhooked
a helmet from the handlebar and pulled it
over her tuque.

"You know how to drive one of those?"
Dave yelled over the roar.

"My dad runs the lifts, remember? I've been
driving these things since I was, like, ten."

I brushed the snow off the other snowmobile, sat down and turned it on.

"Where do we go first?" Hope asked.

I pointed straight ahead. "We go out
that way, straight on the flat area. Then
I say we go up the hill a bit, around behind

the cabin and then downhill a little. If he was walking, he couldn't have gone that far." Dave looked from one snowmobile to the next and finally sat down behind me. I waited for his arms to come around my waist, but he had reached around behind him instead and held the emergency bar. I handed him a helmet. He brushed it off and put it on his head. Hope handed me the extra helmet from the storage beneath the seat of her snowmobile. It felt almost warm as I slipped it on my head.

"If you've been on these a lot before, why don't you go first?" I said.

"Shouldn't we wait for Sam?" Dave asked.

I had seen the flash of the silver flask when Sam disappeared into the bathroom earlier. I had a feeling he wasn't coming with us.

"We'll scout first, then come back and report to Sam," I said.

Hope revved the engine and took off, shooting snow up behind her. I just stared at her until Dave whacked me on the shoulder.

"Go, man," he said. I eased the throttle until we were moving forward. I knew I was being timid, but driving a snowmobile freaked me out. There was a ridge in the snow where the wind had been blowing hardest. I stayed on Hope's trail, though I couldn't see her any longer. We wound in and out of trees, up a few ridges where it took all I had to hold on, and then suddenly we turned up the hill. It was steep. Dave and I had to lean forward to keep from being tossed off. Hope's trail jackknifed back toward the cabin. We leaned into the turn, and I had to slam on the brakes as we came around a little outcropping of trees. Hope was sitting there on her snowmobile, facing us.

"What are you doing?" I yelled over the noise of the engine.

"If he was walking in stuff this deep..." She put her goggles on top of her head and pointed at the snowmobile. "Do you want to turn that off so we don't have to scream?"

"Oh, yeah," I said. I shut the snowmobile down. We all breathed in the silence.

There was a light snow falling and it whispered through the evergreens, catching on branches and leaving the whole area peaceful and calm.

"I was saying, he couldn't have gone farther than this on foot." She pointed into the distance. "And anyway, where would he go?"

"That's what I'm wondering too," I said. "Where would he go?"

"What are you saying?" Dave asked.

"I'm saying someone took him," I said.

"Huh?" Dave said. "Who would take him? And why?"

"I don't know. But what other explanation is there? There's nowhere to go on foot. He left his board. I mean, none of it makes sense."

"But who would take him?" Dave said again.

I thought of everything we knew about Bryce. His family was rich. His dad was a billionaire real-estate developer and big-time adventurer with a fleet of yachts, a private jet and a hot young wife. Bryce had two older brothers. One was a Formula 1 driver, the other played hockey for a team in California. They were both rich and famous. Everyone knew their names. "Well, Bryce's family *is* rich," I said.

"Yeah, we knew that. So what?" Dave said.

"So," I said slowly, "maybe someone kidnapped him, and they're holding him for ransom."

"Whatever," Dave said. "You've been watching too many movies."

"It's possible, Dave," Hope said. "I mean, do you have any other ideas?"

"He wasn't *kidnapped*," Dave said.

"What, then?" I asked. "He sure wasn't, like, suicidal or anything."

"There's got to be some other explanation," Dave said.

Hope took her gloves off, then her helmet. It was warm where we were, sheltered from the wind.

"Okay. Say he was kidnapped," she said to me, ignoring Dave. "Where would his kidnappers have taken him?"

"Down, obviously," Dave said. Suddenly he seemed ready to believe kidnapping was a possibility.

"Why? What's down there?" Hope asked.

"I don't know. Roads, towns, places to go!" Dave yelled.

"Calm down, Dave," I said. "No one's after you."

"I know that," Dave said. "But if Bryce has been kidnapped because his dad is rich, well, what can we do about it?"

"What?" Hope said.

"Well, think about it. What can we do?"

"He's our friend," I said. "If he's been kidnapped, we have to help him."

"And how are we going to do that?" Dave demanded.

"First we have to figure out where they would have taken him."

"We should go talk to Sam. See what he thinks," Hope said.

"He'll think another drink from his flask might magically bring him the answer," I said.

"What are you talking about?" Dave asked.

"Never mind, Dave," I said. "I say we search the area. Sam said there were other cabins around here. Maybe we'll see something. We'll cut through the woods, because, even with the snowfall this morning, there have to be places in the woods where we might see a snowmobile track. What do you think?" Hope was looking at me. Without her neck warmer pulled up over her chin and her tuque yanked down over her head, her green eyes shone in the blue sky. "Well?"

"Sounds good," she said, turning the key on her snowmobile.

chapter eight

We cut back along the mountain toward the woods. I knew what was on the other side of these woods.

The drop.

Hope disappeared in the trees, moving much faster than I was able to. I blamed this on the fact that there were two of us on the snowmobile. But in truth it was because I was still scared of the big heavy machine.

In the woods, Hope's trail suddenly cut up the chute I had come down carrying

Keith Richards. There was more snow here than before. At the same time, the wind had swept clear spots between some of the trees. It was nice in the woods this time. The sun dripped through the tops of the trees, leaving shifting shadows on the ground. The heavy wind had turned into a light breeze. There was a crisp smell of freshly fallen snow. Even the whine of the snowmobile engine didn't bother me that much.

Hope was stopped at the top of the chute. She seemed to be staring at a tree. I pulled in beside her and shut the snowmobile down.

"Someone came by here," she said. "There's a cut in the tree, right there."

"I found Keith Richards over there," I said, pointing to the other side of the chute.

Hope looked at where I was pointing. "The cut is deep here, then shallow here," she said, pointing at the cut again. "It looks like someone took the corner too closely and banged the side of a snowmobile against it."

"That could have been the guys who brought our stuff up here though, right?"

"What guys?" Hope asked.

"The guys who brought our bags and the dummies and the food and all that stuff up to the cabin." She looked at me blankly. "Did you think it was beamed in here or something?"

"I figured the helicopter dropped it all off."

"How?" I asked. "Where would it land?"

"I don't know. I hadn't really thought about it."

"Well, my guess is that there would have been four guys who brought the stuff up," I said.

"Four?" Dave said. "Why four?"

"Think about it. We have two snow-mobiles, which means that there were two people driving them, right?"

"Right."

"But then those two people had to get out of here as well. So there had to be two other snowmobiles to get them back down the mountain. Plus, they would have needed four snowmobiles just to get Hope's bag up here."

"Funny," she said. She swung a leg over the snowmobile and sat back down on it, facing forward.

"Well," I said, "I don't think these trails are from yesterday."

"What trails?" Dave said.

"These ridges, right along the edge here."

"How do you know they aren't from yesterday?" Dave asked.

"I'm guessing, but when I came to the cabin, it was stormy, right?"

"So you said," Dave replied.

"And the wind was blowing straight down this chute," I said.

"So these tracks wouldn't have lasted. They would have been blown away if it had been the snowmobilers who brought our stuff. But the winds last night were blowing across the mountain. That's why it was so hard to get the door of the cabin open. And why there was that long trench in the snow that we just rode along," Hope said.

"Okay. So where do these tracks go?" I asked.

"That way," Hope replied, pointing toward the drop.

"You know what's over there, don't you?" I said.

"We have to go look," she said. "Someone took Bryce, and we need to find him."

Dave muttered something behind me.

"What did you say?" I asked.

"Nothing," Dave replied. "Let's just go." Hope narrowed her eyes at him, put her helmet back on, started the snowmobile and tore off in a great wash of snow.

chapter nine

The drop looked the same as it had the day before.

Terrifying.

Even though there was no wind where we sat, snow was being propelled up and over the rim.

"Wow," Dave said. "Why is it doing that?"

"I don't know," I replied. "But don't get off your snowmobile. I fell in here, and it took me forever to stand back up again. This snow is really deep." The snowmobiles were sunk in the powder. I looked behind us, and our trail was like a ditch on the side of a road. The sun was shining brightly above us. If Bryce hadn't been missing, we'd be off doing our tests to become full-fledged Backcountry Patrollers.

"Can you see any tracks?" I asked.

"Seriously? In all this snow?" Hope looked at me like I was crazy. Or stupid.

"I don't know, Hope. Maybe there's a place where the snow isn't as deep or something? Use your detective skills."

She scowled at me. "The snowmobiles had to come this way. Which means that they could either have gone up, down or over the edge. Up doesn't make sense. I mean, that chute we were in goes to the top of the woods. Why wouldn't you just ride it straight up?"

"And once you got there," Dave said, "where would you go?"

"Well, you could get a chopper to pick you up," I said.

"But we would have heard a chopper. Remember how loud it was? And anyway, in the kind of storm we had last night, there's no way a chopper could have made it in here." I looked down the mountain. The trees went right to the edge of the drop. It would be impossible to get around them.

"They wouldn't have gone down either," I said. "I mean, why come up and then go straight back down there?"

"Exactly," Hope replied.

"So there's only one place they could have gone," Dave said. We all looked at the drop.

"Remember what Sam said?" I asked. "About how you can't tell if the drop is five feet or four hundred feet?"

"I'm not going over there," Dave said. "No way."

"We have to," Hope replied. "Whoever took Bryce went over there. So we have to go over too." She turned her snowmobile back on and started slowly moving toward the edge.

"Don't follow her, Alex," Dave said over my shoulder. "Just turn around. We have to tell Sam what's going on."

"We will," I said, putting my helmet back on. "Just hold on."

"Don't do it, Alex."

"Hold on," I said again. Dave looked at me. His mouth was open a little. His lips quivered.

"I'm getting off."

"Then get off," I said.

"I'm going to tell Sam."

"Then tell Sam," I said. He sat there staring at me.

"I don't think you know Bryce as well as you think you do," he blurted out.

"What do you mean?"

"Before we left, I saw him with these older guys at the lodge. I'd heard about them before."

"What guys?" I said.

"I don't know their names. But I heard they steal snowboards."

"So maybe they'd stolen one of Bryce's boards and he was trying to get it back," I offered.

"Maybe."

"How many times did you see him talking to these guys?"

"Just once." I wasn't even certain that Dave was telling the truth. It all seemed too vague. I figured he was just scared and looking for any reason *not* to have to go closer to the drop. "So, are you getting off?"

In answer, he pulled his helmet back on and reached around for the bar. "All right, hold on," I said.

We crept to the edge of the drop. The snow being flicked up was hard and felt like pieces of rice bouncing off my face. The moaning was loud at the edge. Like a million souls crying out from the depths of hell. Hope was standing up on her snowmobile, slowly moving along the edge. I was impressed. She wasn't showing any fear. She went as far down as possible, then did a half circle and started back up the mountain. As she was passing us, she stopped.

"I can't see anything there," she said.

"I can't either," I replied.

"But there has to be some way down."

I shrugged. "Keep looking, I guess."

The sun had been moving down in the sky for some time, and the light was starting to dim. I pulled my sleeve back and looked at my watch. Almost four thirty. The sun would be setting in the next hour, and then it would be completely dark. I did not want to be here in the dark.

"We only have about half an hour of light left," I said.

Hope nodded and twisted the accelerator.

We drove as far up along the drop as possible and back down again. We couldn't see anything through the snow. In a couple of spots we could see into the distance, where it looked like there were a couple of gentle slopes. But we spent most of our time wiping the visors of our helmets and trying to breathe with our lips tight.

Eventually I pulled up beside Hope. The sun was gone, leaving only the flickering glow of a west-coast sunset.

"We have to go back," I said. "You lead." She nodded, gunned the snowmobile and shot back into the trees. It took less than fifteen minutes for us to return to the cabin, but by the time we arrived, it was pitch-dark outside, and there was still no sign of Bryce.

chapter ten

Sam was asleep on his bunk, his mouth open and pumping out gurgling snores. The air smelled heavily of alcohol.

"Wow. He sure seems concerned for our safety," Dave said. The satellite phone was on the dining table. I picked it up and tried to turn it on.

Nothing.

Hope went into the bathroom. The click of the door closing snapped Sam out of sleep. He sat up and wiped a bit of spittle off his chin.

"Where have you been?" he said.

"Looking for Bryce," I said as I removed my jacket and hung it over the back of a chair.

"You took the snowmobiles. You took off without telling me. You have to tell me when you leave. I was worried."

"So worried you fell asleep?" Dave said.

Sam swung his legs over the side of the bed and stood up. He tilted a little as he stood and then steadied himself. "I guess you didn't find him."

"No," I replied. "And he didn't come back here?"

Sam shook his head.

I was angry with Sam. He was the adult here. He should have been the one out looking for Bryce. He should at least be the one trying to figure out what to do next. He didn't even seem concerned about Bryce. I mean, it seemed pretty self-centered to me. Like this whole Backcountry Patrol thing was just some kind of sideline, a way for him to make money. But didn't he feel responsible for us at all? He walked across the room to the kitchen area. I lit one of the lanterns, and Sam seemed to scurry away from the light. It was almost six o'clock, but in the heart of winter, six o'clock means complete darkness.

"Do you guys want something to eat?" Sam asked. "Pasta? Beans?"

"Pasta," Dave said. "And lots of it. I'm starving."

I was starving as well, but I wasn't going to say anything. I stared at Sam for a minute.

"What?" he said.

"What are we going to do, Sam? We're out here on the side of a mountain. Someone has gone missing. We have no idea where he is, or who took him."

"Whoa, whoa. Who said someone took him?"

Hope had just stepped out of the bathroom. "How else would he have left?" she said. "He wouldn't just go out for a walk and not be able to find his way back, right? We're on the side of a mountain."

"He could have," Sam replied.

"If that's what happened, then why aren't you out going up and down the mountain looking for him? He's *your* responsibility," I said.

"You three took the snowmobiles, remember?" This was true.

"So what's the plan, Sam?" I said.

Water was boiling in a pot on the stove. Sam turned and dumped in some spaghetti, sending hot water splashing to the floor. "Eventually someone will come for us," he said, not looking at us. I thought, That's it? That's your plan? *Eventually someone will come*?

"That's it?" Hope said what I was thinking. She was shaking. "We wait for help? *That's* your answer."

Sam stirred the pasta. "What do you want me to do?" he said, turning to her.

"We have to find out who took Bryce," Hope yelled. "Someone took him over the drop."

Sam squinted at her. "Why would you say that?"

"We found tracks out there. The only place they could have gone was over the drop."

"What kind of tracks?"

"Yeti," I said. "Snowmobile, what else? You do know how rich Bryce's family is, right?

Sam looked at me and shook his head. "Sure, but I never really thought about it."

"Well, think about it now," Hope said. "His dad is really, really rich, and really, really rich people's kids sometimes get kidnapped."

Sam smiled at her. "You guys have some great imaginations."

"Do you have another explanation?" Hope said.

Sam put some pasta sauce in a pot and turned the heat up. He didn't answer Hope's question. And it didn't seem he ever would.

Sam Jenkins might have been great back in the day. He might even have been the best snowboarder that ever lived. But now he was just an instructor who had no idea what to do when trouble hit. Another celebrity who had become so full of himself that other people stopped meaning anything to him.

It was up to us to save Bryce.

chapter eleven

In the morning, as the sun first poked into the sky, I woke Hope up by prodding her in the side with a stick of kindling.

"What are you doing?" she said.

"Get up. We're going over the drop."

"Huh?" she muttered sleepily.

I gently poked her again.

"Stop that. It's annoying," she said.

"We're going to get Sam to show us where it isn't a huge drop, and then we're going over." I was already fully dressed in my snowboarding gear. "We have to get going." She threw her legs over the side of the bed. "And we have to take our boards."

"Why?" she asked.

"Do you want to jump off a cliff on a snowmobile?"

"Whoever took Bryce did."

"Yeah, but they likely knew *exactly* where to go. We'll be guessing."

"But Sam knows," she said. "He told us he did."

"And you trust Sam?" I whispered.

She suddenly had a look of determination in her eyes. "Well, we're going to have to," she said. "At least a little."

"Good," I said. "Because I think you should go first.

Her mouth turned up into a little smile. "I wouldn't have it any other way."

We packed our bags with some food from the cupboard, mostly just energy bars and cereal, and hooked our snowboards onto the racks on the back of the snow-mobiles. I went inside for one more stop in the bathroom. By the time I came out,

Hope had somehow convinced Sam to show us where it would be safe to go over. He still didn't offer to go himself.

Sam drove one snowmobile with Dave on the back. Hope drove the other. The safety bar on the back of the snowmobile was covered by our boards, so I had to wrap my arms around Hope's waist to hang on. I was surprised by how thin she felt. She gunned the engine, and we shot forward. Then she let off the gas, and I was flung forward, my nose sinking into the hair that fluffed out beneath her helmet.

"Sorry," she said. But I didn't mind. She actually smelled pretty nice.

We peeled away from the cabin toward the chute in the woods and then to the drop. We went straight toward it rather than weaving around, as we had the day before. It only took about twenty minutes.

The rushing waves of snow were still washing the edge of the drop. I wondered if they ever stopped. There was almost no wind where we stood. "You shouldn't be doing this, guys," Sam said. "It's just not safe. And anyway, what are you going to do if you find Bryce? Or what if you *don't* find him? Then what? You can't get back up the drop. That's just not an option." He shook his head as he spoke.

"I guess we should just stay in the cabin then?" Hope said. "Wait for the food to run out? Or what's your other idea? Someone will come and find us? There has to be something at the bottom of this mountain. A road or—or *something*." She pointed at the drop. "Just show us where it isn't that much of a fall." Sam looked up and down the length of the drop.

"I don't know," he said.

"Yes, you do," I said. "You told us you did."

"Not exactly," he replied. "I know a general area. But if I'm wrong, you'll just...fall."

"Where?" I demanded. Hope had slid off the snowmobile and unhooked her snowboard. Sam looked up and down the drop again. Then he pointed.

"You can't do this. You could both be killed," Sam said.

"We can't just sit here and wait for someone to find us either," I said. "And anyway, Bryce could be in serious trouble. Don't you want to help him?"

Sam shook his head. He was looking at the drop as though it might reach out and grab him.

"Someone needs to stay at the cabin in case Bryce comes back," he said. He looked sad. As though he wished he was capable of more than he was. Finally he just pointed. "Right there," he said.

"Are you sure?" Hope asked. She had her backpack over her shoulders, her fluffy pink sleeping bag tied to the top. It made her look a foot taller than she was.

"Yeah. Right there. It's probably no more than five feet down. Maybe ten. I think."

"You're not positive?" She had her board on now. I pulled my snowboard off the back of the snowmobile and put my feet in the bindings.

"As far as I can remember. But it's been a long time since I went over there." He looked sad again as he stared at the drop.

I had my snowboard strapped on and was beating my hands together trying to get blood pumping through my body.

"Right there?" Hope said again, staring at Sam.

"Like I said, it's been awhile. But, yeah, I think so." The spot they were pointing at was about fifteen feet down the hill. It looked like any other spot.

"All right," Hope said. Then she clapped her pink gloves together, tightened her goggles and leaned forward to get moving. She did one quick turn just past the snowmobiles and then shot straight past the place Sam had pointed out. She did a quick turn, carved along the edge of the drop, cut out and back in, and then disappeared into the wash of white.

It was entirely silent after she disappeared. Then the moaning started up again. It seemed like the mountain had swallowed her. Sam was just staring at the drop—at the empty space Hope had left behind her.

"Do something, Sam!" I said. "She missed the spot."

"What am I supposed to do?" Sam yelled back.

I climbed up the hill to where Hope had started her run. "We have to go get her."

Sam shook his head. "She made a choice. I told both of you that you were on your own if you decided to go over that drop."

"You mean all three of us," I said. "Right, Dave?"

Dave looked away from me when I spoke to him. He stared at the drop, then up at the sky.

"Dave?" I said.

"I'm not going," he said.

"What?"

"I'm not going over there. I don't even like Bryce. I could get killed."

"You mean you're intimidated by him, Dave. That's the word you're looking for. *Intimidated*."

"No, I'm not. He's a stuck-up rich kid. That's all."

I shook my head and clamped my goggles over my eyes.

"Why should I risk my life for him?" Dave continued.

"Well, I'm going after Hope."

Sam grabbed my arm. "Where she just went off, Alex, it could be a hundred-foot drop. Four hundred feet. You have no idea."

I shrugged his hand off.

"What did you tell us before, Sam? *Don't think, just do it and everything will work out fine.*" I hopped twice to get the snow off my board, then leaned forward. The sun came out and shone on the snow. It felt good to be here. Good to be alive. I turned and aimed myself at the edge of the drop, hoping the feeling would last.

chapter twelve

I considered what my parents would think if they knew what I was doing. I thought about how they would feel if the drop was four hundred feet and they never saw me again. I thought about how much I loved snowboarding and how much it meant to me and how it was all I ever wanted to do. If I were to fall forever, at least I would fall strapped to my board. But I didn't have time to think of anything else, because the drop wasn't any more than five or six feet.

The snow swirled around me as I was in the air, but once I'd landed, it was as clear a day as it had been on the other side.

But different.

The snow was still deep powder, but it seemed lighter. I turned hard back uphill and came to a stop. Looking back at the drop, I could see where the wave of snow came from. There was a long gash in the mountain. In some places, it could have been, as Sam had said, two or three hundred feet down. The gap was never more than ten feet across. In most spots, it was an easy jump. But in others, it really could have been deadly. The wind cut through the drop and pushed straight back up out of it. It was like the wind was riding a half-pipe and just shooting off the lip everywhere it could.

I looked around for Hope but couldn't see her anywhere. It would be easy enough to find out where she was though. Her trail cut deeply through the snow. I took one last look at the drop and turned back down the hill to follow her trail.

It was more wooded on this side. Hope's trail moved in and out of the trees. I wondered why she hadn't waited for me. I hadn't taken that long to get over the drop. Then I came around the side of a tree and noticed that the single trail had suddenly doubled. The trails weaved in and out of each other, making giant figure eights in the snow. Two snowboard trails. It didn't make sense. I slowed down and stopped beside a tree. Without the noise of my heavy breathing and the *swoosh* of snow beneath my board, I was able to hear voices in the distance. It sounded like one person yelling and another responding from farther away. I looked downhill around the edge of the tree. I hefted my backpack tightly onto my back and, going as low as possible, made my way down through the trees.

The two trails split at the edge of the woods. I looked closely at them. One was long and lean—the other more jumpy. The long, clean turns went to the left. The jumpy trail went straight down into the trees. I guessed that Hope had heard the same voices I had and decided to go into the woods to hide. I ducked down as low as I could and followed the jumpy trail into the woods.

The trail cut off just inside another cluster of trees. I turned hard as I spotted Hope crouched down behind a tree in her pink jacket, pants and tuque.

"That is pretty much the worst outfit you could wear if you're trying not to be seen. Unless you're hiding in cotton candy, I suppose," I said.

"Shhhh," she replied. I knelt down with my board wedged into the snow behind me.

"What?" I said. "What are we looking at?" Hope pointed through the trees. A cabin, almost exactly the same as the cabin we had been staying in, was perched on a flat bit of ground. I wondered how these things got up here.

"You think he's in there?" I asked.

"Maybe."

"Hey, whose tracks were those you followed down?" I asked.

"I don't know. I couldn't see whoever it was." Her voice shook a little. With all the bravado she'd recently shown, she was still scared.

But then, so was I.

"That was quite the jump, Hope," I said, in as sincere a voice as possible.

"Whatever."

"No, I mean it. What made you go off where you did rather than where Sam said you should?"

"I think Sam is in on this," she said, not taking her eyes off the cabin.

"What? How?"

"I don't know. Somehow."

"What makes you think that?" There was a bit of wind now, pushing through the trees, making the forest whistle.

"Where he said to go off the landing was all rock. We might have been all right, but our boards would have been a mess. Likely broken."

"Then we'd just be left out there? On the side of the mountain?"

"I guess. I think he's just trying to buy some time. What for, I don't know."

"But how did you know where to go off?" I asked.

"I spotted that area yesterday when we were here. I could see through the snow there. It looked safe enough."

"Safe enough, eh?"

She shrugged. "So what do we do now?"

"I was kind of hoping you'd tell me that," I said.

"Could you see *anything* of the other person who was coming down the hill?"

"Nope." I ducked my head into my jacket. It was getting colder. And being in the shade of these trees wasn't helping.

"I heard someone yelling. Did you hear that?"

"Yeah, two voices."

"Maybe one of them was *inside* the cabin."

"So, two guys then. Could you hear what they were saying?" I leaned forward. My legs were killing me from standing around. Snowboard boots are not the most comfortable footwear. Especially when you've got your feet jammed in bindings.

"Something about someone calling," Hope said.

"Calling?"

"Yeah, like on a phone?" Hope said, glancing at me.

"You think they're phoning his dad about a ransom?"

"Well, duh, of course they are. Why else would they have taken him?" I let her sarcastic tone go. We were going to have to work together here. Not just to get Bryce back, but to get off this mountain alive. I vaguely wondered what my chances of becoming a Backcountry Patroller were now.

"Hope, do you have any idea where we're going to stay tonight?" She didn't look at me. "Hope, it is going to get really, *really* cold out here soon. Where are we going to stay?" She didn't say anything. "Hope do you have a plan at all?"

"Stop saying my name, *Alex*."

"Okay. But do you have a plan?"

"Do *you*?"

I shook my head. "You're the one who went flying over the drop! I followed

93

because I figured you had something worked out. If you don't, you don't. But we have to do something before it gets dark."

She stared at the cabin some more but didn't seem able to say anything. A thought came to me. The cabin here looked a lot like the one we had been staying in. They were likely all the same. Built in some factory somewhere, then air-lifted up here in pieces.

"The cabin has a woodshed," I said. "I think this cabin is the same as the one we were staying in."

"Okay."

"So we can stay in there."

"Without a woodstove?" Hope replied. "We'll freeze."

"I went into the woodshed at the other cabin, and it was warm. The stove is right on the other side. Not like hot or anything, but warm enough. I guess it's set up that way to dry the wood out before it comes inside."

"And you want us to sleep in there?"

"Unless you have a better idea, yeah. This way we can get close to the cabin and— you know—look inside. Back at our cabin, when I was in the woodshed, I could hear people talking on the other side of the wall. Maybe we'll be able to do the same here."

Hope looked miserable.

"Listen," I said. "It's likely our only choice. Even if we started now, we wouldn't make it to the bottom of the mountain before it gets dark. And when we did, who knows where we'd be. Sam said there's nothing around here."

"*Sam said*," Hope repeated. "And you trust him?"

"Not any longer. But we're in the back-country here. It's not like we're going to find a ski village down there. I doubt there would even be any houses." The wind shifted and started blowing up the mountain at us. I unstrapped my boots and sat down on my board. We were in a good enough spot to watch if anyone came or went from the cabin. We couldn't go anywhere until it was dark. I opened my bag and pulled out an energy bar. I offered another one to Hope. Then we sat and ate and waited for the sun to go down.

chapter thirteen

By the time it was dark enough to move, I was frozen. It's okay to be out in those kinds of temperatures when you're boarding. But just sitting around was brutal. The wind had continued to blow all afternoon, sending stinging pellets into our faces.

"We could probably go now," Hope said. It hadn't looked like there was anyone inside the cabin all the time we'd been out there. But when darkness fell, a lantern flicked on inside and we could see people moving past the window.

"We could," I said.

"How?"

"I say we hop up to the top of the tree line and then cut straight down to the cabin. That way we won't ever be visible through the window. The woodshed should be around the other side." I stood up, and my legs complained.

Hope had her arms wrapped around her, but she was still shaking.

"It'll be warm in there. Okay?"

"Okay." I held a hand out and helped her up.

Going uphill on a snowboard is not the easiest thing in the world. You have a couple of options. Take the board off and walk, which always sucks. Or hop up the hill digging your board in with each motion, which is really tiring. Or kind of grapple your way up on your hands and board edge. We used a combination of hopping and scrambling, and ten minutes later we were high enough to get a straight run at the cabin.

"You ready?" I asked. Hope nodded. I jumped a couple of times and then shot out past the end of the woods. As soon as I was above the cabin, I turned and headed straight at it. I could see the woodshed behind. This was good. I could smell the heavy smoke that was pumping out of the cabin's chimney. I leaned a little on my heel side to try and slow down. I switched to my toe side and gently turned back uphill as I neared the cabin, never making more than a light swooshing sound. Then I just drifted backward to the door of the woodshed.

Up the hill, I could see Hope making slow turns. She was standing stiff-legged and straight. The moon was up behind her. I could feel the heat from the woodstove coming through the shed, and my body wanted to simply step inside there and sleep.

Hope began moving down the hill, weaving as she went. The snow was deep enough that she didn't make that much noise. I had just unbuckled my board and was picking it up to step into the woodshed when Hope caught an edge and went flying off in the wrong direction. I almost yelled at her, but stopped myself just in time. She spun around and then tried to dig in her toe edge, but nothing seemed to be working for her. She shot way out, cut back in and slammed straight into the door of the cabin.

I froze.

"What was that?" someone inside said. There was the sound of scuffling. I looked around the corner of the cabin and saw Hope sprawled out on the ground, struggling under the weight of her backpack. She looked up and saw me. The door to the cabin opened, and she waved at me to hide. I grabbed my board, took two big steps through the snow and opened the door to the woodshed.

"Who are you?" a man's voice said from the front of the cabin.

"Where is Bryce?" Hope yelled. There was a long pause. I stepped inside the woodshed. It was warm, and light leaked through from the main cabin.

"You're here to save your little boyfriend, are you?"

"He's not my boyfriend," Hope replied. "What have you done with him?"

There was another pause, then the man's voice again. "Oh, you'll see, little girl. Come on, get up." It sounded like Hope put up a bit of a struggle. The man grunted a couple of times, and Hope screamed. Someone else was called to help, and soon there was silence again.

The woodshed was big enough to move around in, but not much more than that. The wood was piled about two feet from the back wall. I slid my board in behind the pile and sat down beside it. If anyone came, I could get in behind the pile. It smelled damp and heavy. I leaned my head against the wall.

"Yeah, a girl," I heard someone say. The voice was close. Whoever was speaking must have been putting wood in the stove. "I don't know. I'll take the sock out of her mouth and ask her." There was a muffled response. "Hope. Hahahaha, yeah, her name's Hope."

I couldn't hear anyone else speaking, so the man must have been talking on a satellite phone. "I know. I guess we can leave her here." There was another long pause. I put my ear to the wall. "Okay. I don't like it, but I guess we have to do what we have to do." I heard the door of the woodstove slam shut. Then the man's voice faded away until I couldn't hear him at all.

Now what was I supposed to do? If I went crashing into the cabin, I'd be in the same boat as Bryce and Hope. But if I sat out here, who knew what would happen to them. I looked at my watch. It was almost nine o'clock. The sun was down, and the air was crystal clear and thin. I watched my breath form a cloud before me in the flickering light that leaked from the cabin.

Okay, I thought, they can't possibly be going anywhere until morning. What I need to do is sleep. My job here is to be well rested. Have an active mind. Be able to focus. And in the morning, something will come to me.

I looked at the woodchip-covered ground. Something scurried in the corner. I decided it was worth the risk to get my sleeping bag out. I unrolled it on the floor and was about to climb inside when I had a second thought. Wouldn't it suck if someone came in here and I was asleep on the floor in plain view? I pushed my pack behind the wood pile and slid my sleeping bag in after it. Then I climbed inside and closed my eyes. This was going to be one of the worst nights of my life.

chapter fourteen

I hardly slept that night, though I guess I must have drifted off eventually. I was awakened by a log falling on my legs. I almost yelled. Then I remembered where I was.

Through the woodpile, I could see a tall man in a North Face jacket bundling logs into his bent arm. A cigarette jutted out from one side of his mouth, and he was squinting against the smoke. He dropped the logs, swore and bent over to pick them up. If he had looked forward rather than down, he likely would have seen me. I didn't move. I tried not to breathe. I held my head still and stared at the man, willing him to simply walk out the door and into the storm. He got three logs up into his arms, then dropped one of them. He cursed and pulled the cigarette out of his mouth. I couldn't tell how heavy he was, because his jacket and snow pants were large and puffy, but he seemed huge. He puffed on his cigarette a couple of times, looking around the small space as though there might be something of interest there. Then he flicked the spent cigarette out into the snow, bundled the logs up into his arms again and kicked the door open. A terrible wind was blowing. Snow was whipping up into the air and then curling and rolling away. The man leaned into the wind as he kicked the door closed.

I sighed and stretched out in my sleeping bag. I hoped that would be the last time someone came out for wood before I was out of there.

"Not human out there," someone said inside the cabin. I heard the logs drop to the ground in a clatter followed by the bang of the woodstove door opening. "Call him and let him know that we might have to delay."

"We can't delay," someone else said. The voices were so muffled, I could barely tell one voice from another. "We might not have an option. If the weather doesn't change, we'll have to stay."

"We *can't* stay," a third voice said. "Call him, see what's happening on his side of the mountain."

"You think it's going to be any different over there?"

"Just call and see." I waited a long time to hear something else. But nothing came. I was extremely hungry. If my stomach made any more noise, the kidnappers would hear it. I quietly opened my backpack and dug through it until I found an energy bar.

"It's clear," someone said. "He says it's clear over there."

"Then we go. Call your guy and set the coordinates for a pickup spot."

"We still have to get out of here," someone else said. "And what about the girl?" I hadn't heard anything from Hope. But if they were talking about her, she must be all right.

"We can just leave her."

"No, we can't. She'll follow us."

"Then we can tie her up in here."

"No. What if no one comes this way and finds her? You can't control that kind of thing."

"I don't know! When this is all over, we can call someone and let them know."

"It's not that easy." I still couldn't really tell if there were two or three people talking. Before, I'd been certain I'd heard three distinct voices. Now I wasn't so sure. "We shoot her," a different voice said. Definitely three people, then. There was no response. Why was there no response? There were only two rooms: the main space and the bathroom. So Bryce and Hope must be locked up in the bathroom.

I slipped out of my sleeping bag, rolled it up and stuffed it in my backpack. I kept my ear to the wall, waiting for an answer. No one was going to shoot Hope, I told myself. That wasn't going to happen.

The door to the woodshed suddenly shot open. I froze behind the pile and waited, but no one came in. The door slammed shut.

"What was that?" one of the men asked.

"The door to the shed. I must have forgotten to latch it," another man replied.

I sat back down and ate my energy bar.

"...the storm is coming in..." I heard through the wall. "...says we have to go now or never." The woodstove banged and there was a long hiss. I could smell smoke, and soon its wispy fingers were floating into the shed.

"Leave everything here. Just get the boards ready."

"What about the girl?"

"She comes with us," came the response. Two other voices said, "No."

The door opened again. The wind howled in the shed, and I couldn't hear anything from inside the cabin.

I pulled my snowboard out from behind the woodpile and strapped my backpack over my shoulders, all the while waving smoke away from my face. If I stood at the door of the woodshed, I could see downhill. Whoever was inside would have to go out the door and then straight down. Especially if they were on boards. So unless they looked back, which no one ever really does on a snowboard, I would be fine to follow them.

I strapped my board on and waited. About five minutes later, the first person popped into view and started down the hill. Close behind him was Hope. Then Bryce. Then another man.

But where was the third kidnapper? I was pretty sure I had heard three male voices. I waited and waited. I couldn't see the group anymore, and the storm was closing in. I had to go, or soon I wouldn't be able to follow their tracks. I jumped forward. Then I grabbed the side of the house and shoved as hard as I could. I kept the board flat, which is never a good idea, but I keep my board well waxed, and this was the best way to pick up some speed in the deep powder.

I crouched down, tucked as much as possible and waited for a bullet to go through my head.

It took less than a minute to get into the woods. I glanced back and couldn't see any movement in the cabin. Whatever the third kidnapper was doing, he wasn't looking out the door or window. Or maybe he had been. Maybe he had seen me and was using a satellite phone to call ahead to the others. There was no way of knowing.

The trail went through the trees in a kind of sideways shuffle. I followed, moving as quickly as possible but keeping my eyes peeled for the last man in the group. I suspected that they would be going fairly slowly. The weather conditions were bad and getting worse.

The trail cut out of the woods and onto a steep, open slope. I came to the top of this section and stopped. The wind was blowing straight across the slope, making it almost impossible to see anything.

Or anyone.

I looked down at the trail in the snow. It appeared that the boarders had cut across the hill, back toward the other side of the mountain. But this didn't make sense. The drop went from high to low. We were on the low side. It wasn't possible to make it back up, was it? Or maybe the drop didn't go all the way down the mountain. We had never asked Sam about this.

I dropped into the downhill. I was trying to look as far forward as possible, but it was getting more difficult to see anything at all. The trail moved steadily sideways, every so often dipping into steep downhill rolls.

Ahead of me there was nothing but white. Everywhere, everything was a solid white. The trail had disappeared beneath me. I couldn't tell which way the others had gone.

I stopped and listened for voices, but all I could hear was the howling wind. I cut back down again, figuring that they would keep going down and over until they came to the drop.

I did this for about two minutes until the slope flattened out. Then I went more directly down, picking up speed. I did a couple of quick turns, all the while trying to see through the storm. It felt like I was picking up too much speed, so I cut hard on my toe edge and shot back up the hill to stop and look. As I was turning, readying myself to drop in on my heel edge, I heard a scream.

A girl's scream.

chapter fifteen

I didn't even think about it this time. I just dropped back in and tucked as hard as I could toward the sound. I hadn't gone more than twenty feet when I spotted someone. It looked like one of the kidnappers. The one who had been at the back of the group. I decided I would try and run right into him. If I could take him by surprise, then I'd have the upper hand. I tucked hard and aimed straight for him. But just as I was gaining on him, he did a quick jump and steered himself down the hill. I got close, but the element of surprise was gone.

I finally discovered what this area of the mountain was like. There was a split in the mountain, much like the drop, and we were on the low side of this. However, there was a massive wall of snow shooting up into the air at an extreme angle. It was like a launch pad that, if you hit it just right, would launch you up and over to the other side of the mountain. The kidnapper tucked at it, rode up the side and shot into the air. He just managed to clear the lip of the other side. I had no choice but to follow him. I shot into the air, pulling my legs up tight beneath me, and just managed to creep over the lip on the other side. I was so close behind the kidnapper that I almost landed on him.

"What the...?" he yelled. I peeled off and cut up the mountain.

"Where is Hope?" I shouted. "And Bryce?"

"Another one!" he replied. "Your little girlfriend is hanging on over there," he said, pointing back where we'd just come.

"What?"

He laughed and disappeared into the storm. I headed for it. I could just make out something pink on the edge. I headed for it. As I got closer, I could see Hope hanging on to a rock, her bottom half dangling over the edge. There was no launch pad here. Just an open, immeasurable nothingness beneath her.

I skidded to a stop, lying down as I did so, and dug my board into the snow. I grabbed Hope's arms.

"Stay still," I said. I started to pull, and my board shifted forward. I dug it more deeply into the snow and pulled again. Hope didn't weigh much, but with the board on her feet, it was like dragging an elephant up the side of a skyscraper. I pulled as hard as I could, and she moved another inch or two.

"Is there anything you can get your board on?"

"No, there's nothing here." Her voice was higher than normal.

"Swing a little. Just try." She shifted around, and it was really hard to keep hold of her. Her jacket was slippery, and so were my gloves. "Hold on to the rock again," I said.

"No. Don't let me go."

"I have to get a better hold on you, Hope. Just hold the rock for a second."

"No, no. Please don't let me go."

"Okay. Try this." I was panting as I spoke. The strength was being sapped from my arms. "Grab the rock with one hand. I'll still have a hold of you."

"No, no, no."

"Hope. You have to do this. I can't hold on much longer." She looked up at me. Her face was red. There were cuts on her cheeks and nose. Her eyes looked desperate and lost.

"Trust me, Hope. It will be okay. Just trust me." Tentatively, slowly, she let go of my arm and grabbed the rock with her right hand. I quickly shot forward and got my arm under her left arm. Now her face was beside mine, my elbows dug hard into the packed snow.

I looked down and couldn't see the bottom. Just a foggy haze of snow and rock.

"How far is it?" Hope asked.

"Don't worry. Don't look."

"How far?" Her breath was on my cheek.

"Hope, you're going to have to drop your board. It's the only way I'll be able to pull you up."

"But how will I get down the mountain?"

"It's the only way. Do it now." She slipped a little, and I steadied her. She gasped in my ear. "Please, Hope, do it now." She let go of my arm with one hand, reached down and undid the front binding. With a little wiggling, she was able to get the back binding undone. Somehow she managed to pull the board up and toss it over the edge of the lip. It dropped into some deeper powder, then slid down the hill.

"How did you do that?"

"Just get me up," she yelled back.

"Okay," I said. "On three. One, two, *three*." I pulled hard, and Hope came up over the edge. I pushed her forward, and she scurried into the deep snow. There were tears streaming down her face. She had more thin cuts on her face from where she had slammed into the edge of the cliff. There was blood coming from the cuts and dripping on the ground.

"They tried to kill me," she said. I was still lying on my front in the snow. It was difficult to even move. My arms felt limp, solid, almost dead.

"What happened?"

"I came over the edge there, and no one..."

"What?" I yelled into the wind. Hope crawled over to me and put her face close to mine.

"They came over the edge of that last descent, and everyone just shot for the ramp or whatever that thing is. No one told me I would have to jump. Alex, I wasn't even close to ready."

"But everyone else made it fine?"

"Yeah, like they'd done it before."

"Even Bryce?"

"Well, you know Bryce," she said. "It's not like anything would surprise him." The wind was pushing what felt like shards of glass into my face.

"We have to get off of here," I said. "Before we freeze."

"Where did my board go?" she asked. I couldn't see it, but there was really only one option.

"Down," I replied. I looked at the slope beneath us. It was steep, and the powder was loose. I undid my bindings.

"Sit up here," I said, pointing to a spot just in front of the front binding. Hope clambered over without a word. I got on behind her and started pushing. Once we hit the steeper bit of the slope, it was easy enough to slide down.

Stopping was the only real problem.

chapter sixteen

I dug my heels in as we approached the trees, but it wasn't enough. The snow just bundled up around my legs. Hope jammed her legs down as far as they could go, but that didn't help either. We were heading straight for a large evergreen.

"Jump!" I yelled, grabbing Hope by the shoulders and shoving her off the board. We both sank into the snow and came to a stop. My board, on the other hand, rode on top of the powder until it hit a tree. Then it did a giant flip and landed upside down.

"That had better not be broken," Hope said.

"Just get into the trees," I yelled. We scrambled through the waist-deep snow. It was like swimming in Jell-O. It had warmed a little, and the snow was already becoming spongier. We finally managed to get into the wooded area. Hope leaned against a tree, exhaled and began to cry. I looked around and found her board where it had stopped and put it at her feet.

"Please don't cry," I said, before I realized how insensitive that would sound. "I mean, it's all right, Hope. We'll get out of here."

"How do you know that? We're all alone up here."

I thought about that for a moment. "No, we're not," I replied.

"Who else is here?" She looked hopeful.

"Sam and Dave," I said. Then, "And the third guy in the cabin with you."

"What third guy?" Hope asked. She had a glove off and was wiping the tears from her cheeks.

"When I was in the woodshed, I could hear three people talking."

She shook her head. "No, just two."

"What?" I had distinctly heard three voices. "What about Bryce?"

"He was there too."

"Just there? Not handcuffed or tied to a chair or anything? Did he say anything to you?"

"No. The kidnappers stuffed me in the bathroom and tied me to the sink as soon as we got into the cabin." That seemed strange to me. If Bryce had been kidnapped, wouldn't they have tied him up like they had Hope?

"So what are we supposed to..."

"Shhhh," I said, holding a hand up. I could hear something.

Rumbling.

Like giant rocks knocking together.

Like an avalanche.

"Hope," I said. "We have to go." My eyes must have been huge and filled with fear, because Hope immediately began to panic.

"What? Why?"

I grabbed her board and put it in front of her. "Fast," I said. The rumble was getting louder. An avalanche takes out everything in its path. Depending on how big the avalanche was, this little forested area we were in could be flattened in a matter of seconds. The week before, we'd watched a video of an avalanche. When the video was over, no one said a word. It was one of the most frightening things I'd ever seen.

"Avalanche, Hope," I said, grabbing her foot and jamming it into the binding. She looked uphill.

"Where?"

"It's coming. I can hear it." The ground shook. "I can feel it." We were in a spot just beneath a steep slope. With the angle of the hill and the weather, we couldn't see much farther than a hundred feet up the mountain. The avalanche would be on us before we knew it.

Hope got her other foot buckled in. I jumped through the snow to where my board had landed and quickly checked it for damage. One of the edges had popped out slightly, but it was at the rear and faced backward. As long as I didn't do a 180 out there, I'd be fine.

"Go," I said. The rumble was getting louder and louder. I expected any minute to see a great wave of snow flowing down the hill. I gave Hope a push to get her started. She shot out ahead of me. I slammed my boots into the bindings, grabbed a tree, pulled myself back and shot forward. I went into a tuck right away and caught up with Hope before we were out of the wooded area.

"Tuck," I yelled. She bent down over her board and leaned forward. I scanned the area beneath us, looking for a spot where there was some kind of tunnel in the ground. We'd been told to look for a ditch— an area that was lower than the rest of the mountain—if we were ever caught in an avalanche.

And then to stay out of it.

Get up on the top. As high up as possible. You cannot outrun an avalanche. It's impossible. Your only real choice is to head for higher ground.

This part of the mountain was a straight shot though. There was nothing we could do but go down. Hope did a wide turn, trying to slow down.

"Hope," I yelled. "Straight. No turning."

"I can't!" she screamed back.

"You have to. We can't slow down." The rumble was deafening. It sounded like a herd of buffalo chasing a mass of rhinos down the mountain above us. Hope cut back in front of me and settled into a tuck. I knelt, keeping as low to the ground as possible and leaning hard over the front of the board.

And then I looked behind me.

chapter seventeen

The avalanche had crested the slope and was overtaking the wooded area we'd just traveled through. The trees bent to the ground as the great wave of snow washed over them.

"Go!" I yelled at Hope again.

"Where?"

"Straight." The avalanche was catching up with us. It was only a matter of a minute or so before it would be on us. All I could think of was all that snow on top of me.

Forever.

Not being able to breathe beneath its weight. Or being dragged down the mountain like a surfer dumped on a reef and then sucked into shore.

I started scanning the area beneath us again, trying to find a spot where we could get up and above the wash of snow and debris.

But there was nothing. Nowhere to go but down.

We entered another circle of trees. This time it was mostly evergreens. We were getting to the base of the mountain, but because of the storm, I had no idea how close we were. Absolutely everything was white.

Snow began to pass beside us and beneath our boards. The center of the avalanche would be on us any second.

The slope turned slightly, banking first to one side then the other. At the second corner, there was a ridge. It must have been twenty feet high. The avalanche could wash right over this, or it could follow the cut of the mountain and keep going. We didn't have a choice though. We had to try.

"Hope!" I yelled. She couldn't hear me. The roar of the avalanche was all around us. Inhaling all sound. Taking everything that got in its way to the base of the mountain. I tucked up beside her and pointed at the ridge. She shook her head. I pointed again.

"It's our only chance," I yelled.

"I can't get up there," she yelled. I clasped my hands behind my back.

"Tuck," I yelled. "And when you get to the lip, just launch. Just jump! You can do it." She looked at the launching area as I shot ahead. I couldn't help her any more than I just had. She was going to have to believe in herself now.

The side of the hill seemed to be mostly ice from where winds had whipped across the slope and pushed the snow into giant piles. With sections like this on mountains, the other side is often a straight drop as well. I came in at an angle, then cut hard up the side like I would if I was going to launch off the wall of a half pipe. When I hit the top, I pulled my legs up and grabbed the base of the board. I landed, pushing hard on my heel edge, then flipped over onto my stomach and watched Hope shoot up the wall. The avalanche was right behind her, rolling along the side of the ridge. I could make out everything from the logs of a cabin to trees and rocks rolling in the avalanche's wake.

"Pump, Hope. Pump!" I yelled. She didn't look behind her, which was a good thing. She focused on the lip. The avalanche washed up to the top of the ridge and grabbed the back of her board just as she was about to take air. It shot her out horizontally. I reached out and grabbed her as she flew past. Her speed dragged us both sideways. I slid along the top of the ridge until I could dig my board into the snow. Then we stopped, and I held onto Hope with all I had.

"Hold on," I yelled. She screamed. My arms felt like they were going to be ripped out of their sockets. But if I let her go, she'd be washed down the ridge and rolled into the mess of snow and debris. My board slipped, and Hope screamed again. I looked up the mountain. Snow was pouring over the top of the steep area above the trees. I couldn't see any more than the tips of the trees now, and they were all pointed downhill. It was like nothing I'd ever seen before. The simple power of snow rolling down a hill.

Hope dug her snowboard into the ridge and started pulling herself up. I pulled as hard as I could. As hard as I ever had. She popped up onto the top of the ridge and looked down over the other side.

"That is a *long* way down," she said. The final bits of snow trickled down the mountain. Everything beneath us looked different. There were trees dropped on the trail. Rocks, even boulders, were strewn about the space. Hope leaned over and kissed me on the cheek.

"Whoa," I said.

"You saved me. Like, twice in the last half hour."

"You're welcome."

She leaned her head into my chest and stayed there, shaking. I put an arm around her.

"I want to go home," she said eventually. So did I.

"Let's get down to the bottom of the mountain," I said. "Then we'll see where we stand. There has to be a road down there. And Bryce must be somewhere." She nodded and pulled herself away from me. Then she wiped her face, pulled her goggles back on and stood up.

"Let's go then," she said.

"All right," I replied. "We'll have to cut back down that way. It's too steep here." I hopped back a few steps and looked at the drop in. "We'll get some good speed here." I looked out across the slope. "So cut that way. It looks less wooded. We can't be that high up any longer. We should be able to get down in the next hour."

"That long?"

"I don't know," I replied. "Once we get off this ridge, try to stay beside me."

She looked like she was going to say something sarcastic and then decided against it.

I got myself to a spot where it looked safe to drop in.

"Ready?" I asked.

"Ready," Hope replied. I was about to jump up to clear the edge and start down the slope when I heard someone yelling.

"Help, help! He has a gun!"

chapter eighteen

I could just make out Dave popping over the edge of the slope above the woods. He was moving extremely fast.

"Duck," I said to Hope.

"Why?"

"Someone has a gun." A second later, Sam flew over the edge, tucking down toward Dave.

"That's Sam," Hope said. "And it looks like he's chasing Dave!"

"Wait until they get closer," I said. "Then we're going to follow them."

Dave was screaming. He was also snowboarding better than I had ever seen him snowboard before. Fear will do that to you, I guess. But Sam was better. Sam was better than all of us.

"Why would Sam be chasing him with a gun?" Hope asked. As they passed beneath us, I could see the gun in Sam's hand. "Okay, let's go," I said. I jumped as high as I could, shot myself forward and out and landed cleanly on the ridge. I took one quick backward glance to make certain that Hope had made it before dropping into a tuck and following Sam's trail. The mountain was fairly open—especially after the avalanche had flattened everything in its path. I was following their trail, but Sam and Dave would pop up on a ridge now and then. Dave seemed to be boarding all over the place. Cutting from side to side, then going straight down. Like he expected Sam to fire a bullet at him. He was screaming as well. His voice echoed off the peaks around us.

I took another quick look back. Hope was close behind, carving beautiful lines in the snow. I smiled a little and thought of the kiss on the cheek. Then I tucked hard, rode up on my front side edge and went as fast as I could down the mountain. I had a plan on how to get Sam. To save Dave. And maybe even find Bryce.

It took a couple of minutes, but with Dave weaving all over the place, it was easy enough to catch up to him and Sam. I waited until the last second, hoping that Sam wouldn't see me. Luckily, he was focused on Dave. The gun he was holding looked strange. It was short but had a very large barrel.

"Stop, Dave!" Sam yelled. "It's not what you think." He turned one way, then the other, and as he was about to turn back onto his heel side, I went straight into him, jumping a little as I did so. He went down hard in the snow, and it was all I could do to stay upright. I landed sideways, spun out, hit the ground with my arms outstretched and then bounced back up again as I came to a stop.

The gun had flown out of Sam's hand and was lying between the two of us. Sam looked at me. There was a bit of blood coming from his nose. His eyes were wide and his mouth slack. Just then, Hope came up behind him.

"Grab the gun," I yelled. Sam looked over his shoulder, and Hope curled around him, went down low and snatched the gun out of the snow.

Dave had stopped beneath us, yelling. "He's with them! He's in on it."

Hope stopped beside me and handed me the gun. It was huge. On the side it said *Flare Pistol*.

"What are you doing, Sam?" I said.

He shook his head. "It's not what you think."

"Are you in on it?" I said. "Are you in on the kidnapping?"

He shook his head again. "No. It's not..."

I pointed the flare gun at him. "This likely won't kill you, but it will *really* hurt. We'll leave you up here, Sam."

"It wasn't supposed to go this way," he said. "It was all Bryce's idea."

"What?" Hope said. "He wanted to be kidnapped?"

"Yeah. He did."

"Why?" Hope said. She didn't look like she believed anything Sam was saying. Sam wiped a bit of blood from his face, then spat into the snow. "And for once, Sam, tell the truth."

The wind had died down, and we were able to speak to one another without yelling. Sam took his sunglasses off and dropped his arms at his sides.

"He wanted to prove something to his father. That's what he said, anyway."

"Who? Bryce?"

"Yeah, Bryce. You know how his brothers are such big deals. Hockey star. Race-car driver?" Sam shrugged. "And as cool as being in Backcountry Patrol is, it doesn't really match up with driving four hundred miles an hour or being named the NHL's MVP. I guess his father kind of looks down on him. So Bryce wanted to make his father sit up and take notice. To see him as being an equal to his brothers. So he decided to prove to his father how smart he is. He might not be an MVP or win

Formula 1 races, but he could pull off a kidnapping scheme against his own father."

"How would that work?" I said. It didn't make sense. "Byrce is an amazing snowboarder. I mean, why not just become a professional? Wouldn't that impress his father?"

"Compared to his brothers, he would still be nothing. That's what he believes, anyway."

"An Olympic medal might work," I said.

"Listen, Alex, I know you love snowboarding. I know you think it's the greatest thing in the world. And, hey, I agree. But what are the chances of an Olympic medal? He'd be lucky if he got a good sponsorship and maybe a few grand when he wins a contest. Not as impressive as his brothers, that's for sure."

"So he did it for the money?" I was not understanding this. Sam looked at the sky.

"He told me he thought it would make his father see him differently. See him as someone intelligent enough to pull off a kidnapping, extort money from him and get away with it. Maybe it will, who knows. Or maybe it won't. At the very least, he will have his father's attention. And maybe that's all he wants." Sam grabbed the back of his head. "Man, you really hit me. Why'd you do that?"

"You had a gun!" I yelled. "You were chasing Dave!"

"I just didn't want him to get messed up with those guys. Those are, like, bad guys."

"But you were working with them?"

He shook his head. "Not really. Bryce came to me and told me what he was going to do. I told him it was stupid and then..." Sam looked at the sky.

"And then Bryce said he'd give you some money if you helped him out."

"Well, yeah. That was part of it."

"What was the other part?" Hope asked. Sam looked down at the blood-sprinkled snow. "Come on, Sam. We have the gun here. Tell us what you know."

"Bryce had found out something about me that I'd rather people didn't know."

"What?"

"The reason I disappeared." He looked up again, though this time his eyes were directed toward the mountain. "I lost a friend on this mountain. A good friend. He wiped out on a ledge, and I wasn't able to save him. I wasn't able to do anything at all for him. He died out here."

"But there would be reports and everything from that, right?" I said.

Sam shook his head. "I never told anyone we were here."

"What? You left your friend out here to die?"

"He was dead." Sam stared at me. "He was dead with his board on his feet, and that's all that mattered. He was doing what he loved. My friend, Mike Carolina, wanted to be the best snowboarder there was. And it killed him. He didn't have any family. No sisters or brothers. His parents had died years before. Mike had this, this *drive* to just go that step further. To prove something. And it killed him."

I could understand why Sam had never told anyone. This kind of information could ruin him in any number of different ways. At the very least, he would be fired as a Backcountry Patrol trainer. It explained a lot as well. His disappearance for all those years. The flask he kept in his pocket. Losing a friend that way must have been incredibly difficult. Even so, he should have told somebody what had happened.

"How did Bryce find out?"

"I don't know. Sometimes when I drink, I talk too much. He might not have known everything, but he knew enough. I'm thinking of making a comeback. That kind of information would kill it for me. And I didn't do anything wrong. I left my friend right where he would want to be. This whole mountain is his coffin."

"What about the kidnappers?"

"They got in contact with me. I didn't really have to do anything."

I shook my head. Then I opened my jacket and put the flare gun inside.

"You believe him?" Hope said.

"I do."

"Why?"

"Because I remember when he was on the circuit. Other riders said he was the best.

But they also said he was the most honest. Back in the day, there were different ways down a mountain. You could cheat. Sam never cheated in a competition. Not once."

"No," Sam said. "Not once."

"And remember what Dave said before about Bryce hanging out with those guys who steal boards?" I said.

"Those are the guys," Sam said.

"And Bryce wasn't tied up in the cabin," Hope said. "I should have known."

"So how do we get him back?" I said.

"What's going on up there?" Dave called up from below.

"We'll be there in a minute, Dave. Just chill out," Hope said.

"I heard him talking on the satellite phone with them!" Dave yelled. I looked at Sam.

"Yeah, that happened."

"So the phone wasn't broken?"

"No. That was a bit of a lie. I kind of took the battery out."

"But it doesn't matter, right? Because Bryce will be fine? These guys'll just hand him over to his father?"

"That was the plan," Sam said, standing up. "But the plan has changed."

"How so?"

"They want to keep the money. So now they've actually kidnapped Bryce."

chapter nineteen

"So what do you think they'll do now?" I asked.

"They wouldn't tell me. They just said I'd been paid. That my part was done."

We boarded down to where Dave stood. He stared at Sam.

"I heard him on the phone with the kidnappers," Dave said. "He's in on it. What are you doing with him?"

"It's not that simple, Dave," I said.

"It seemed that simple to me. He is in on it."

"Listen, these guys weren't going to kidnap Bryce. Bryce *wanted* to be kidnapped. He set the whole thing up. But now they actually *have* kidnapped him."

"What?" Dave said.

"Sam explained it."

"Of course he did. Don't believe him. I heard him on the phone. And you should have seen him last night."

"What?" Hope asked.

"He was drunk. He thought I didn't notice."

I didn't even look at Sam. "It doesn't matter, now, Dave. We have to save Bryce."

Dave gave me a funny look. "Who made you boss?"

"Stay here then. I don't care." I turned back to Hope. "So what do we do now?" The storm had passed. It was almost three, and the sun was still high in the sky and warm. If we had had nothing else on our plates, a nice day of boarding would have been ahead of us.

Instead, we were trying to save a friend from a mess he'd got himself into.

"Sam," Hope said, "where were they supposed to meet this car?"

"At the bottom," Sam said.

"Yeah, but where?"

"There's a logging road that winds along here. The car was going to pick them up at the northern tip. That's why they called before. They needed directions."

"All right," Hope said. "Do you still have that phone?"

"Yeah," Sam said, digging around in his jacket.

"Okay, here's the plan. But we have to work fast."

The plan was simple enough. Sam called the kidnappers and told them that he had some information about the pickup. That someone knew. That he couldn't talk on the phone because the line wasn't secure. He told them to stop and wait for him.

The kidnappers said they would wait, but we couldn't trust them. We had to get to the car before they did, or the rest of the plan wouldn't work.

"They have a major head start on us," Dave said.

"Yeah," Sam replied. "But they had to wait out the avalanche. On the phone, they said that someone had gone down and they were trying to dig out his snowboard. If we go fast, we'll beat them to the bottom. I can call my friend, the pilot, and get him to bring some police out here." Sam looked at the phone. "I don't have much juice left though. This'll be the only call I'll be able to make. Then we'll have to hold the kidnappers off until the police show."

"All right," Hope said, taking control again. "You and Dave go that way and try to follow them. Alex and I will shoot straight down and get to the car. When we get there, we'll take care of the driver. You guys be ready to do something with the kidnappers."

"Listen to her," Dave said. "Take care of the driver. What are you, a gangster?" Hope leveled a cold stare at him. She put her goggles on, and a second later she'd jumped into the air and was tucking down the mountain.

"See you on the other side," I said, as I leaned into the hill.

"You go," Sam replied. "Clean up this mess." I was twenty feet below them when I heard Sam yell out, "Be safe, man."

I tucked hard down the mountain, making long turns when I had to. The avalanche had flattened everything out for us. It was like riding down a construction site at times though. At one point I noticed a woodstove stuck against the side of a tree. It looked like the one from our cabin. It would have made me laugh at just about any other time.

I caught up with Hope, and we boarded side by side for a while. Then we came over a ridge and could see the logging road in the distance. It was flat and wooded. It was a welcome sight, all that flat land.

"Go over there," I said, pointing to some tall trees that had survived the avalanche. Hope cut hard to the right and I followed.

Once we were stopped behind a tree, I said, "Look for a car."

The sun was coming in hard from our right. We cupped hands above our eyes and started to search the land beneath us.

"Right over there," Hope said. I looked where she was pointing. A car was parked beside some trees at the bottom of the hill. Someone was standing beside it.

"How do we get down there without whoever that is seeing us?" I asked. Hope took a glove off, undid the zipper of my jacket and reached inside.

"How far do these things shoot?" she asked, pulling the flare gun out.

"A long way, I think. It's a flare. You shoot it up, and it explodes."

"Think you can make it down the hill a bit farther?" Hope asked. "Just down to those other trees. Without being seen?"

"Sure," I said. Though I was far from certain.

"You get down there, then I'll fire this across the slope. When whoever it is down there looks at it, you tuck down and hit the bank in front of him. Do what you did to Sam." I squinted at the man and the car and wondered if what she was suggesting was even possible. "Then I'll come down with this, and we wait in the car for the rest of them."

"You really think that'll work?"

"I don't think we have any other options." She was right. And if Sam and Dave had made it to the other kidnappers, then they'd all be on their way here.

"All right." I did a quick turn, knelt down as far as I could and started through the trees.

It still scared me to weave through wooded areas. That hadn't changed. And going through them in a crouch was really difficult. I couldn't see where my line should be. I couldn't even tell if my next turn might be into a tree.

After about two minutes, I cleared the first section of trees and broke into the second. I stopped and waved at Hope. I couldn't see her, but she was up there. Watching. The car was an old Honda Civic, the rear license plate dangling from one screw. A man was leaning against the car, right beside a mass of snow left behind by the avalanche. If I went down just right, I could hit that mound of snow and launch straight into his chest. I wasn't worried about hurting him like I had been with Sam. If I knocked him out, so much the better.

I looked back up the hill just as the flare shot out of the woods. As we expected, the man looked toward the explosion rather than to where it had originated. I pushed hard off a tree and aimed myself directly at him.

He never saw me coming. I hit the mound of snow and went out and up. I grabbed the front of my board right between my feet. When I hit him, it was with the full base of my board on his chest and shoulders. He disappeared beneath me, and I leaned forward to dive across the roof of the car. I came over the other side, spun off and landed hard. It knocked the air out of me, and I lay there for a minute, sucking at nothing and feeling like my chest had collapsed. Everything went white for a minute and then black. I closed my eyes. Had I broken something? I wanted to feel my body, to touch my arms and legs, but I couldn't breathe.

Something inside me didn't seem right. I could feel the cold ground pushing through my snow pants. What a day, I thought. I opened my eyes and looked up at the blue sky. The clouds had parted, but there was a cold wind running down the mountain. Everything rolls down that mountain, I thought. Wind, snow, sunshine, people.

Suddenly Hope's face was over mine.

"You knocked him out cold," she said. I tried to smile. "You okay?" I widened my eyes at her and continued to try and suck air. "Breathe," she said. "Inhale, exhale, inhale." I listened to her voice and tried to do as I was told. I couldn't speak. Couldn't even move. Slowly, I began to feel better. I was able to take a breath and sit up.

"We have to get him in the trunk before he wakes up," Hope said.

"What?"

"We can't just leave him sitting there. Come on." She was down on one knee, undoing my bindings.

I stood up, which was a challenge. My legs felt like lead as I followed Hope to the other side of the car. The guy was out cold on the ground. A big purple bruise was starting to spread across the side of his face. Hope grabbed his feet.

"That was awesome, Alex. I've never seen anything like it." She had already popped the trunk. "Come on, let's get him in. Can you take his arms?" I reached down.

It hurt.

It really hurt. There were flashes of white and big black holes everywhere. "Are you okay?" Hope said.

"I don't know," I replied. "Something really hurts."

"Just get him in the trunk, and then you can lie down." I felt dizzy, but somehow I managed to pick the man up. He was light, which was good, and we didn't have far to carry him. We dropped him in the trunk, and Hope slammed the lid closed.

"Come on, lie down on the backseat." She helped me into the car. I lay on my back, looking at the peeling material of the ceiling. It smelled like cigarette smoke and greasy fast food. Hope slid into the passenger's seat.

"You don't look so good, Alex," she said. "Can you hear me?" I nodded. But her voice was coming and going. She turned away. All her movements left a kind of hazy trail behind. The last thing I heard was her yelling, "Drop that gun. Drop it, or I'll blow your head off!" And I thought, Wow, what a crazy girl.

chapter twenty

Hospitals are always so white. Even when they paint the walls, it still *feels* white. Or green. But that sick-looking green.

When I returned to the land of the living, a man in a long white coat had his hand down my top.

"Wow!" I said, inhaling hard. Which I shouldn't have. Because inhaling hurt. "Why does that hurt so much?" I asked. The man in the white coat didn't say anything for a moment. Then he pulled the stethoscope away from his ears.

"Because you have a collapsed lung, young man," he said. "You are very lucky."

"Am I?" I asked. I didn't feel lucky. I felt like I was going to stop breathing at any moment and not start again.

Which might be okay, because if breathing hurt this much, maybe I should just quit it.

There was a shuffling in the room. I watched Sam rise from a chair behind the doctor. He had stubble on his face, and his eyes were bloodshot.

"Sam," I said. "What are you doing here? Actually, what am I doing here?"

Sam laughed and reached out a hand to me. "Man, you hit that guy hard. Don't worry, though, the police were looking for him anyway. He'll be in jail a long time, thanks to you. Then you stuffed him in a trunk? With a collapsed lung? That is hard-core."

"I stuffed someone in a trunk?" It came back to me in a flash. The whole mess from beginning to end.

"Yes," Sam said, laughing. "Yes indeed, my man."

"Is Bryce all right?" I asked.

"Yeah, man, he's fine. His dad came and got him." He shook his head. "I don't think that is going to go all that well."

"No?" I replied.

"People have to accept that they are who they are." Sam stared at the window for a minute. "Never try to prove to people that you're something other than who you are, Alex. Just be the best *you* you can be." He laughed. "That sounded dumb."

"It sounded true, Sam," I said. "What about you?"

Sam looked across the room at a man I hadn't noticed before. A cop. "I have some explaining to do," Sam said. "But I convinced them to let me stay here until you woke up."

"But you weren't really a part of it," I said.

Sam shrugged. "Don't worry. I'll be all right. And hey, now that you're an official member of Backcountry Patrol, we'll need you out there soon."

I smiled. Then the police officer took Sam by the arm and led him out of the room. Hope stepped inside as the door was closing.

"You're all right," she said. I shrugged, which hurt more than it should have.

"So are you," I said. "What happened?"

"Well," Hope replied. "You crushed a lung, dumped a criminal in the trunk of a car, and then I finished off the hard work."

"Which was what exactly?"

"Convincing the kidnapper to drop his gun."

"And how did you do that?"

"I said I'd shoot him," she said with a smile.

"Okay, but he had a gun too, right?"

"Sure, but he wasn't too worried about a girl in a puffy pink snowsuit. Big mistake." She blinked a few times. "Those guys are amateurs. They were in over their heads. The guy with the gun dropped it like he'd had enough. Like he'd been waiting for this to happen."

I could imagine.

"Taken out by a little girl," I said.

"Little girl?" Hope said. "No. He was taken out by an official Backcountry Patroller." She sat down in the chair beside my bed. She looked very different out of her snow gear. She looked like an actual girl. Enough that I almost forgot how annoying I'd once found her.

Hope looked out the window at the light rain that was falling on Vancouver.

I thought for a moment about what to say next. "You know, you were pretty amazing out there."

"Thanks," she replied. "So were you."

"Would you actually have shot him?"

She looked at me as she considered her answer. "You know what? After all we've been through? I think I can pretty much do anything now."

"Anything?" I asked.

"Yeah," she said, looking me right in the eye. "Anything." And I didn't doubt her for a second.

Acknowledgments

I would like to thank anyone who ever said, "You can do it," even if they didn't mean it. Shout-outs go to my past writing "coaches," Rick Taylor, Tom Henighan and Paul Quarrington, and to my friends and first readers, Sarah Leahy, Mark Molnar, Nichole McGill, Ros Paterson and Sylvie Hill. Thank you also to my editor, Sarah Harvey, who molded a jumble of sentences into something that makes sense. Finally, thank you to anyone who is reading this. Keep reading. Oh, and thank you to my grandmother, who will be 103 this year and will read this book. Twice. That's just how she rolls.